Nightmare

Vampire
Blood

"*May I have the next dance?*" *asked the vampire in a silky voice.*

"*You aren't Cos!*" *cried Ari.*

"*No,*" *said the vampire.* *I'm not.*"

Ari's eyes opened wide. In the shifting light, she thought she recognized the face from her vision – the tightly drawn white skin and aquiline nose, the dark, glittering eyes of her nightmare.

"*But can't we dance anyway?*" *suggested the vampire, his voice sweet. He reached out and she felt his cool hand on the back of her neck. She tingled from head to toe and felt vaguely sick as he took her in his arms and guided her into a slow two-step. Her head felt fuzzy and she was having trouble thinking clearly. The figures around them seemed to fade and grow dim.*

"*Tell me about yourself,*" *he said softly.*

Lions
An Imprint of HarperCollins*Publishers*

More heart-stopping Nightmares . . .

and soon to come in the Vampire Twins *trilogy*

2 Bloodlust
3 Bloodchoice

NIGHTMARES

Vampire Twins 1

BLOODLINES

Janice Harrell

Lions
An Imprint of HarperCollinsPublishers

First published in the USA in 1994 by
HarperCollins Publishers, Inc.
First published in Great Britain in Lions in 1994

1 3 5 7 9 10 8 6 4 2

Lions is an imprint of HarperCollins Children's Books,
a division of HarperCollins Publishers Ltd, 77-85 Fulham
Palace Road, Hammersmith, London W6 8JB

ISBN 0 00 675087 7

The author asserts the moral right to be identified
as the author of the work.

Printed and bound in Great Britain
by HarperCollins Manufacturing Ltd, Glasgow

CHAPTER
ONE

MRS. MONTCLAIR PALED AND CLOSED THE NEWSPAPER hastily. Paul took the paper from her hands and scanned the headline. "Jeez," he said, "the serial killer is at it again."

"Creepy!" said Anne-Marie. She dipped a scoop of mashed potatoes, dented it with her spoon, and neatly dribbled gravy into the dent.

Paul frowned at the newspaper story. "It's kind of weird. All of them have bled to death, but the cops don't find the bodies in a puddle of blood or anything. The guy must kidnap them, take them somewhere else to slit their throats, then dump the bodies on the street."

Mrs. Montclair took a long shuddering breath. "Paul, do you have to talk about this now? Why can't you read the comics like other kids?"

Paul tossed the paper aside. "I don't know what you're worried about, Mom. It's always drunks he goes after. I mean, half the time they find the bodies right outside a bar. That tells you something, doesn't it?"

"Nope," said his sister. "You just said they couldn't have been killed near the bar—else there would have been lots of blood around. So he could have kidnapped them somewhere else."

"Yeah, right," said Paul. "For your info, Ari, they always print the alcohol content of the corpse, and lots of times these guys were drunk."

Anne-Marie's name was always shortened to Ari because that was as much as she could manage when she was small. At sixteen, the nickname still stuck. She rested her chin on her hand. "It's funny the way he kills them. Why not just shoot them? Maybe he's got a sick thing about liking the blood."

The saucepan slipped from Mrs. Montclair's fingers with a clatter and gravy spattered the floor. "That's enough!" she cried, stooping to wipe it up with a paper towel. "I don't want to hear another word about this deranged killer." Her voice shook. "Not a word, do you hear me?"

Ari and Paul glanced at each other and shrugged. They knew from the tone of their mother's voice that she meant business. Paul flipped to the comics and did not glance out the kitchen window that gave onto the dark backyard.

Outside, a shadowy cloaked figure darted with swift, fluid movement up onto the Montclairs' back porch, then tiptoed up to the open kitchen window. He gripped the window frame tightly with his pale hands and peered hungrily in at the twins and their mother.

"What's that?" he heard Ari cry.

"Nothing," Paul said, glancing at her. "Calm down."

The vampire drew back at the sound of the twins' voices. Then silently he stepped down off the porch. The print of his hand glowed phosphorescent on the window frame for some seconds. The garden gate creaked as he let himself out of the yard. In the next garden, a dog yipped. The vampire cringed and thrust his hands deeply into his pants pockets. Moving slowly, he made his way out to the sidewalk.

On either side of the old street in New Orleans's French Quarter, town houses rose tall and gray in the semidarkness; scaffolding and ladders threw spidery shadows onto the broken concrete. The vampire whistled a monotonous tune under his breath. Suddenly, a man in a raincoat stumbled into the lamplight. He smelled of liquor and his grin was vacant. The man grabbed at the lamppost to steady himself. "Oops!" he mumbled to himself. "Steady now. Take it easy, Cholly-boy. Let's get home in one piece, hey?"

"Excuse me," said the vampire courteously. "Can you tell me the time?"

The drunk fell into peals of laughter and slapped his thigh. "Man, I thought you were going to ask for a light. That's what you're s'posed to ask for. A light. Like they do in the movies. Don't you ever go to the movies?"

The vampire recoiled for a moment. The street-lamp showed the glossy white of his handsome face, its aquiline nose with the flesh drawn tightly over the bone. "No," he answered softly. "I don't need a light. Only the time, if you please."

"Sure," said the drunk. "Jusht a minute, man. Hang on." He shot his cuff to expose his watch, but he had no chance to speak. In a movement almost too fast to see, the vampire buried his face against the man's soft neck. With an impatient toss of his head, the vampire tore the flesh. The carotid artery spurted violently, and dark blood spattered the vampire's face. The vampire pressed his lips tightly against the man's neck and sucked greedily. His victim slumped and the vampire made a quick gesture of impatience and let him fall to the cement. The man's head lolled to the side, and in the lamplight, his open eyes were lifeless. Glancing around first to be sure no one was watching, the vampire dragged the body between the houses and let it slip to the ground. Most of the corpse was hidden in shadows. He glanced down at the trousered legs and brown shoes that pressed against a clump of rank weeds. Fastidiously, he wiped the sticky blood off his lips and cheeks with a corner of his cape. Then he smiled. In the weak light of the nighttime street, his pale face appeared almost to have taken on the glow of life. He thrust his hands once more into his pockets and walked off whistling.

Moments later, a neighbor knocked at the Montclairs' front door, and Ari ran to open it. The

4

neighbor held out a folded newspaper. "Congratulations to your mom on her promotion, Ari. I saved this for you in case she wants to send a clipping to the kinfolk."

"We didn't even see the story, Mr. Wilson," cried Ari, taking the paper. "Thanks. I'll show Mom. Want to come in?"

"Nah, I've got to be getting back."

Ari smiled. "Well, thanks again."

In the Montclairs' kitchen, the twins and their mother pored over the section of paper the neighbor had brought. "It was nice of George to bring it over," said Mrs. Montclair.

Ari dimpled. "He said he thought we would want to send a clipping to the kinfolk. He doesn't know that we don't have any kinfolk."

"Unless you count Aunt Gabrielle," said Paul.

"I don't," said Ari promptly. "One Christmas card a year? That's not real kinfolk."

Paul threw his arm around his sister, and they burst into song. "We are po-ooor little lambs," they crooned, "with no kinfolk."

Their mother covered her ears. "Stop! Stop!" She laughed.

Paul made a sad face. "Our own mother thinks we can't sing. We must be bad."

"Very bad," agreed Ari.

Their mother blushed. "I never said you couldn't sing," she said.

"It's okay, Mom. We know we can't carry a tune, don't we, Ari?" Paul looked down at his sister. He was taller, but except for height the twins

5

were as alike as bookends, with dark hair curling slightly at the temples, fair skin, and dark, fringed brown eyes.

The phone on the wall rang and Ari grabbed for it. "Speak for yourself, Paul." She stuck out her tongue. "I'm planning a singing career." Then into the receiver she said, "Hullo? Oh, hi, Laurie. Wait a minute. I'm going to switch to the phone in my room."

Once Ari had gone to her bedroom, Paul picked up the receiver.

"Hang up, Paul!" his mother insisted.

Paul covered the receiver with his hand. "Heck, Mom, Ari knows I listen. She doesn't care."

"A young woman is entitled to some privacy," said his mother firmly. "You two are not children anymore. Now hang up."

Paul shrugged and strolled out of the kitchen. When he got to his room, he smiled to himself and quietly picked up the receiver on his bedside table. His mom didn't understand the first thing about being a twin, he thought. She couldn't seem to grasp that he and Ari shared everything.

"And take out the garbage!" his mother called after him. "Now!"

Paul put the phone down and groaned. Reluctantly, he went out to the back porch and lifted the black plastic liner out of the can. Outside, the cool night air was rich with the familiar scents of the neighborhood—fried fish, the fresh bread smell that came at night from the big ovens at the bakery. But also on the breeze was the scent of garbage and the vaguely ominous smell of the cold stale water in a nearby pond. Behind the lot, black leaves rotted, and pond beetles skimmed the water.

Paul twisted a tie around the top of the black plastic bag, hoisted it, and made his way down the wooden steps. In the next garden, a chain rattled and a dog whimpered. Paul kicked the garden gate open and backed out. The overstuffed plastic bag banged against his shins and caught on the gate latch. Paul heard it rip. "Damn," he said, wrenching the bag free. Once he had squeezed through, he kicked the gate shut behind him. He could smell the crushed ragweed under his sneakers as he backed toward the street. Tired of carrying it, he let the bag drag on the ground, hoping it wouldn't split. He hated taking the garbage down the narrow, weed-clogged passageway between the houses, but his mother wouldn't think of letting him take it through the living room.

Suddenly, Paul's foot struck something and he turned, startled. A chill slithered up his back when he saw the dark shape at his feet. Headlights from a passing car cast a sudden moving light on the gaping mouth and pale face of a man whose head was only inches from Paul's foot. For an instant, Paul was half-blinded by the sudden light. The next moment, the car disappeared down the street, and the dead man at his feet was again swallowed up by the shadows.

Paul gulped and tried to speak, but at first nothing would come out. "Are . . . are you all right?" he whispered, kneeling. He had only meant to touch the man's shoulder, but he lost his balance and fell against him. The stranger's head rolled to the side. When Paul pulled away from the man, he realized, horrified, that his hand was damp and sticky.

He backed away and fell against the garbage bag. Scrambling to his feet, he ran to the garden gate and raced up the porch steps. The dog next door howled mournfully, but Paul scarcely noticed. He was dizzy and a loud noise roared in his ears. Somehow he made it to the door and an instant later, stumbled into the brightly lit kitchen. He stood still a moment, breathing heavily. The kitchen clock hummed quietly. He reached out for the counter to steady himself, then turned on the tap and furiously began washing the blood off of his hands.

Ari stepped into the kitchen, twirling a strand of long dark hair around her finger. "Guess who Terry Hobbes has a crush on?" she sang. "Me, me, me, that's who. He asked Laurie if she thought I liked him. What do you think about that?"

Paul turned off the tap and stared at her in disbelief. She seemed to come from a different, more sunlit world. "Ari," he whispered, "there's a dead man outside. I touched him."

Her jaw dropped. "Are . . . are you sure?"

"I kicked him with my foot," said Paul. "I was carrying the garbage out, and I kicked him and he never moved, not even when I fell against him."

Mrs. Montclair appeared white-faced at the open kitchen door. "What are you saying, Paul?"

8

"We'd better call nine-one-one," said Paul. "There's a dead guy right at our gate."

"Maybe he's only passed out," said Mrs. Montclair. "I'll call an ambulance."

Paul exchanged a glance with Ari. He didn't have to say anything, because Ari could read the grim meaning in his eyes. The man was dead, all right. Paul reached into the kitchen drawer and pulled out a large flashlight. Behind him, he could hear the phone beeping one high note and two low as his mother dialed 911.

"Don't you dare go back outside, Paul Montclair!" his mother cried. "Don't you move!"

Paul stepped onto the porch and Ari followed him. He could hear his mother speaking excitedly to the 911 operator as Ari closed the door.

"You better go back in," Paul told his twin. "Mom's about to have a heart attack." He felt the familiar wooden steps under his sneakers as he played the beam of the flashlight nervously around the overgrown garden in their narrow, fenced backyard. Long shadows leapt to life, and scraggly bits of greenery were bleached by the flashlight's beam.

"You're not going by yourself," said Ari, clutching his arm. "What if the murderer is still out there?"

Paul licked his dry lips. "Who said the guy was murdered?"

"You know I can read your mind, Paul." Ari tightened her grip. "Don't try to pull anything over on me." It was a long-standing joke between them that they could read each other's minds. Sometimes, they actually could.

Paul played the flashlight once more over the yard. No one seemed to be hiding in their garden. But in all the darkness and shadows, who could be sure?

His stomach squeezed painfully when he thought of the corpse, but he made himself push the garden gate open.

Ari slipped through the gate after him. Paul aimed the flashlight at the ground, and the weeds became a nightmare of shadows. Suddenly the strong beam of light rested on the man's face. The corpse's blank eyes gleamed in the light, then the beam wobbled. The flashlight rattled to the ground and went dark.

"He looks dead to me," said Ari, shivering.

"He is dead," said Paul. "I shone the light right in his face, and his pupils didn't contract."

"Let's go inside, Paul. I feel sick."

Her twin picked up the flashlight and restlessly clicked its switch several times. "Damn. It's broken." Paul heard the distant sound of a siren. "Did you see whether there was any blood on the ground?" he asked.

"I don't think there's much blood," she said, clinging fearfully to her twin. "The weeds looked dry."

"There's blood on him, Ari," said Paul. "I got it on my hand."

"Paul? Ari?" Their mother called out the back door.

Ari jerked at Paul's arm. "Let's go inside," she

10

said. "We can't see anything out here now anyway."

Reluctantly, Paul followed Ari back through the garden gate. He wished he hadn't been so shaken as to drop his flashlight. Now that he could hear the siren growing closer, he wasn't nearly as afraid of what might have been lurking in the shadows. It would have been exciting to get a better look at the murder scene.

Their mother, her brow furrowed anxiously, stood at the back door. "The police are on their way. What are you two doing out there? Trying to scare me out of my wits?" She shooed the twins back into the kitchen and locked the door.

Paul walked into the living room. The siren was wailing close at hand now, and he could see a flashing blue light outside. "They're here. I'd better go show them where the body is," he said.

"Paul!" wailed Mrs. Montclair. "Why can't you stay put?"

"Don't you understand, Mom?" asked Paul. "It's as close as we'll ever get to a real murder investigation. If I hadn't broken the flashlight, Ari and me might even have found a clue."

Shadowy figures mounted the steps on the front porch. There was a rap on the door, and Paul opened it. Two uniformed policemen confronted him. "We got a call from this address," said an officer.

"I'm the one that found the body," Paul told them. "I was taking out the garbage, and I ran right into him. I'll show you."

Paul led the police officers to the side of the house. The rotating blue light cast an unearthly glow on the shadowed corpse. A policeman switched on a flashlight and played its beam over the dead body.

A wave of nausea swept over Paul when he saw that the man's shirt was spattered with dark red blood. "I've never seen a dead person before," he whispered.

"You better go inside, son," said one of the officers. "Just give your name to the officer in the patrol car."

Paul went out to the street and gave his name and address to the officer in the patrol car. "Do you think it's the serial killer?" Paul asked the officer.

"Can't say at this point. But don't you worry. We'll take care of it."

Paul cast a regretful glance over his shoulder but reluctantly went up on the porch. The police didn't seem to be doing a very good job of tracking the serial killer. According to the newspaper, they didn't have any leads.

The shadowy figure of the police photographer knelt beside the body. A flash briefly whitened the murder victim's face.

One of the officers stepped up to the side of the porch and fixed a thin yellow tape to the bannister.

"Do you think it's the serial killer, Officer?" asked Paul.

The officer glanced up at him. "Hadn't you better go inside and do your homework?" The police officer strung the yellow tape alongside the porch. He pulled it out as far as the street and tied it to the lamppost. "POLICE LINE—DO NOT CROSS," it said.

Paul's mother plucked at him. "Let's go inside, Paul. You heard the man. They don't want us out here." An ambulance pulled up before the house, and the attendants slid out a stretcher.

Paul hesitated. "Heck, Mom."

"Inside," she commanded.

Reluctantly, Paul obeyed. Ari had pushed the curtains aside and was staring out at the shadowy uniformed figures of the police officers.

"Get away from that window, Anne-Marie Montclair," said her mother.

Paul's gaze met Ari's. They could see that their mother was upset. Paul realized that he didn't feel exactly calm himself.

"Well, it is creepy," Ari murmured as they followed their mother to the kitchen.

"Nah, it's like a movie," said Paul in a low voice. "The body didn't even look real. His face was dead-white, like plastic."

"You were pretty shaken up," argued Ari. "You dropped the flashlight, remember."

Paul recalled the bony slackness of the victim's jaw. "I guess it was kind of sickening," he admitted.

Mrs. Montclair poured herself a cup of coffee with a shaking hand. "Kids, we may have to move out of town."

Paul and Ari stared at her in amazement.

"But what about your promotion?" protested Ari.

"Mom, crime happens everywhere," said Paul. "Nobody picks up and moves these days just because

13

one body is dumped in their neighborhood."

Mrs. Montclair ran her fingers frantically through her gray-streaked hair. "We'll talk about it later. I have to think about what's best for the entire family. We . . . we may have to go far away quite suddenly. I'd rather you didn't mention it to any of your friends. Or anyone else, for that matter."

The twins glanced at each other anxiously. What was she talking about? She sounded completely crazy—moving and not telling anyone? How could the dead body bother her that much? Paul had the sudden, awful sensation that their secure world had begun shifting under their feet.

Later that night when Ari had gone to bed, Paul crept into her room. "Ari?"

"I'm awake," she said. She scooted over in the bed to make room for him.

Paul slid in under the covers. "What do you think is going on with Mom? I know she's been jumpy lately, but tonight she's completely losing it."

"A dead body would upset anybody," said Ari.

"I know. That's what I figured at first, too. But think about it—she didn't even see the guy. And it's not like it has anything to do with us. If the serial killer did it, that means the guy probably wasn't even killed in our neighborhood."

"I wish you'd quit reading that stuff out of the paper about the serial killer, Paul. Mom hates hearing about it. And now look what's happened. He dumps a body on our street, and all of a sudden she's talking about moving."

Paul shivered. "Well, naturally, I never figured he was going to strike right in our own neighborhood."

"Maybe she'll calm down if we don't mention it anymore," suggested Ari.

"That's what I think," said Paul, relieved. "Boy, she scared the heck out of me. Moving! It's crazy!"

"We'll pretend she never mentioned it," repeated Ari. "Don't bring it up."

"Don't worry! Jeez, did you hear her? 'Someplace far away.' Sounded like she was talking about Oregon or San Diego. I'd hate those places."

"All our friends are right here in New Orleans," said Ari in a small voice.

"She can't be serious," said Paul. "She just got that big promotion." He hugged his twin. "We won't let her do it. It's two against one, remember? We'll make her see it our way."

"We stick together no matter what happens," said Ari, squeezing him tightly.

"We're not leaving New Orleans!"

"Never!" cried Ari.

"I feel a hundred percent better," said Paul. "I swear, it beats me why people who aren't twins don't go nuts." Smiling in the darkness, he slipped out of her bed and tiptoed back to his own room.

CHAPTER
TWO

THE NEXT MORNING IN THE TWILIGHT BETWEEN WAKING and sleeping, Paul sensed the presence of his father. It was as if inexpressible warmth and bright happiness were almost within his grasp. He felt his father leaning over him, breathing on him. His longing was so strong that he was sure he could he reach out and touch him. But when he awoke, he saw only the cold washstand beside his bed, the first rays of light glittering on the white enamel pitcher. He felt a thud of disappointment, coupled with a nagging uncomfortable sensation that he had misplaced something important. He did his best to push the feeling away.

Paul went in the bathroom, splashed cold water on his face, and got dressed. As he was buttoning his shirt, he walked into the living room and glanced out the window. A stiff breeze blew a cellophane bag along the street, and the yellow plastic tape the police had strung around the scene of the crime flapped in the wind. If it hadn't been for the tape marking off the space between the houses, Paul might almost have imagined the dead body was another of his strange dreams. Now that it was daylight, everything that had happened the night before seemed unreal.

When he had finished getting dressed, Paul went downstairs to the living room. He noticed something on the floor—an envelope that had fallen from the trash can by his mother's desk. He bent to pick it up. It was addressed to "Ms. Mary Ellen Montclair" on Rampart Street. The broad sweeping strokes of the handwriting, faintly reminiscent of his aunt Gabrielle's script, made Paul catch his breath sharply. The support checks from his father always came with no return address on the envelope. He squinted at the postmark but could not make it out. It was always the same. There was never any clue where the envelopes were mailed from. Paul dropped it back into the trash. Then he pushed back the curtains and gazed out the window. He knew he had to quit thinking about his father.

The body had been removed by the police, but the black plastic bag of garbage still lay in the weeds. Paul wondered how long the garbage would lie there rotting. He couldn't take it out to the curb now because the area between the houses was roped off by the yellow police tape, and no one was supposed to cross that line. The day was heavily overcast, and the scene outside looked somber and gray.

Ari came out of her bedroom and stretched. Paul's eyes softened as he looked at her. Her straight dark eyebrows matched his, but everything else about her was nicer. She was beautiful. Her face was flushed with sleep, and her cheek still bore the mark of a crease from her pillowcase.

"Mom not up yet?" Ari yawned.

"Nope."

The twins heard their mother's alarm go off. That meant their mother would be appearing soon. Paul plucked the envelope from the trash and showed it to Ari.

She looked frightened. "Paul, you're not going to talk about Dad, are you? Mom's already upset."

"No, I'm not going to talk about Dad. But don't you wonder where he is, Ari?"

She hesitated. "No."

"Liar," he said amiably.

"Okay, sometimes I do wonder. A little. But he's never going to come see us. Never. All these years and not a single birthday card, no Christmas present—I don't even remember what he looks like."

"I figure he must look sort of like you and me," said Paul. "Mom's not dark the way we are."

Ari cast an anxious glance over her shoulder. "If she hears us talking about him, you know it's going to make her sad."

Paul glanced down at the envelope. When he read it, the letters swirled and danced with color, but when he held it too far away to read, he could tell the ink was black. He couldn't remember when he started seeing letters and numbers in color. Sometimes it slowed him down when he was doing math problems or reading. Sea green, baby blue, tangerine, he would think, dazzled by the color of the letters and numbers. No one else seemed to see them that way—not that he had asked. He hadn't even mentioned it to Ari. What if it meant he had some kind of slow-growing brain tumor? He quietly dropped the envelope back into the trash. "Okay," he said, his face expressionless. "Let's get breakfast."

The morning paper had a brief mention of the murder. "SERIAL KILLER STRIKES AGAIN." Paul and Ari usually divided the paper in the morning, Paul taking the front page and Ari the inside section and comics, but when they saw the ominous news on the front page, Ari silently folded the paper up and hid it under the telephone book.

In the weeks that followed, the police removed the yellow tape, the garbage was carried to the curb, and Paul was careful to avoid mentioning the serial killer. He was relieved that there had been no more discussion of moving, but he sensed that murder was never far from his mother's mind. She had floodlights installed on the back porch, and she began to insist that Paul take the garbage out to the curb before dark. He noticed that she made excuses to keep him and Ari from going out at night.

But Paul didn't argue with her. The truth was he wasn't that eager to go out after dark himself.

He couldn't shake the feeling that a killer might be waiting for him in the shadows.

"Mom is still really nervous," Ari murmured one evening. She glanced sideways toward the living room where their mother had gone to bolt the front door. "And it's been weeks now since you found that body." She got up and stared out the window in the back door. "Paul!" she said softly. "Someone's out there!"

He jumped up and ran to the door. Transparent figures moved beyond the windowpane, a blank-faced boy and someone shorter standing beside him. For a minute Paul's heart stopped, then suddenly he laughed. "It's our reflections, Ari!" His voice was shaky. Paul lifted his hand and the transparent ghostly hand on the window rose to meet it.

Ari clutched him. "Is that all? Are you sure there's no one outside?"

Paul flicked off the light in the kitchen. Standing in darkness, with no reflections on the glass, he could see outside. The porch floodlights threw a path of light onto the worn wooden porch and lit up the stepping-stones and, farther back, a forlorn cracked birdbath. Beyond that lay profound darkness. Paul knew that past their neglected garden lay the stagnant pond surrounded by a tangle of live oaks, vines, and undergrowth. How could he tell Ari that nothing was out there? Anything could be hiding in the dark mass of vegetation.

"Someone is out there," said Ari in a low voice. "I know it. And he's looking for us."

Paul felt the hair on the back of his neck prickle. He teased Ari about being overimaginative, but amazingly often her sixth sense turned out to be right. Maybe there *was* someone out there.

The wall switch clicked and the kitchen was flooded with light. "What are you two standing here in the dark for?" cried Mrs. Montclair shrilly.

Paul gulped. "We were only taking a look outside, Mom. The new floodlights work great. We can see halfway to the back fence."

Mrs. Montclair closed her eyes. "If we lit up this entire quarter like a football stadium, it still wouldn't be bright enough for me," she said. "All these dark old houses, the shadows under the balconies, the walled gardens. There are altogether too many places around here where someone can hide."

"You used to love the French Quarter," said Ari softly.

Her mother stared at her blankly as if she hadn't heard. "Don't you think it's time you kids got down to your homework?" she asked.

The twins looked at each other in dismay. Since they found the body, there'd been no sign that their mother was calming down.

The next day, Paul found a typed business envelope with an Oregon postmark in the mail. The postmark jolted him.

21

"Let's steam it open," he suggested to Ari.

"But that's so sneaky!" cried Ari. "We ought not to read Mom's private mail."

"It's our lives we're talking about," said Paul. "Mom won't be home for hours. Don't we want to know what's going on? Are you ready to move to Oregon?"

Reluctantly Ari put a pot on the stove and turned on the burner. When steam began to roll from the pot in puffy clouds, Paul held the envelope over it until the adhesive loosened. Then he carefully slipped his fingers under the envelope flap and lifted it open. The twins read it together. "Thank you for your inquiry about the position of station manager," it began.

They stared at each other. "She's already applying for jobs out of state," whispered Ari.

"We've got to glue this envelope shut," said Paul. He got some white glue from the desk and squeezed some on the flap.

"Don't put too much on it," warned Ari. "We don't want it to look gloopy."

By the time Mrs. Montclair got home from work, the glue on the envelope was dry. She ripped the envelope open and read the letter with excitement. Ari glanced at Paul. He looked so guilty that she was sure her mother would guess what they had been up to. She looked down and buttered her soft roll. "Ann Hendricks says she thinks I've got a good chance at being newspaper editor next year," she said.

Mrs. Montclair slid the letter back into its envelope. "Don't make too many plans for next year, Ari. You remember I told you we might have to move."

The twins gazed at each other in dismay. "But we love it here!" protested Ari. "We don't ever want to move, do we, Paul?"

Paul shook his head.

"Things don't always go the way we would like, sweetheart." Mrs. Montclair made a wry face. "I'm sure you'll both make friends wherever we go. And don't forget we've got each other." She avoided looking at them. Ari knew it was because she hated to see them unhappy.

Ari wanted to scream, "Look at me! See the tears streaming down my face. See what you're doing to me! I can't move in the middle of my junior year!"

Mrs. Montclair pushed her chair away from the table. "I'm going to have to be away for a few days to go to a job interview. Maybe you can stay with Laurie, Ari. And Paul might like to stay with one of his friends."

Ari and Paul exchanged a panicky look. "Laurie can put us both up, Mom," said Ari. "I can sleep with Laurie and Paul can sleep on the couch the Bergers have in the den." Ari couldn't be separated from her twin now when so much was going wrong.

"If it's okay with the Bergers, it's fine with me," said Mrs. Montclair. "But please don't let on that we might be leaving town."

"You mean not even tell Laurie?" asked Ari in amazement.

23

"Not even Laurie," said her mother. "We . . . we may need to make a clean break of it. Luckily, the post office has a new rule that they don't give out forwarding addresses. I want to keep this move a secret. I know I can count on you both." She hastily turned on her heel and left the room.

"Does she think I'm going to move and not even mention it to anyone?" asked Ari.

The twins sat in silence. A moment later their mother swept into the kitchen. "I have to run to the grocery store before it gets dark." She smiled at them tremulously. "Now, don't worry, kids. We're going to be fine. It will all work out." When she bent to kiss them, Ari smelled the faint scent of peppermint that clung to her.

A minute later, they heard the front door of the house close behind her.

"Maybe she won't get the job," said Paul.

Ari was too choked up to speak. Leave her friends? Her mother couldn't be serious!

The twins heard the crunch of metal on metal and ran to the living room window. Mrs. Montclair's blue Chevrolet had locked bumpers with the neighbor's car. Their mother stood in the street pantomiming dismay while Mr. Wilson, dressed in a business suit, stood on the locked bumpers. Flinging his arms in the air, he bounced. At last both cars rocked free. Ari and Paul could see their mother's lips moving, but they couldn't make out what she was saying.

"And she has the nerve to call me a bad driver," said Paul. "I bet she wasn't looking."

Ari let the curtain drop. "Anybody can see she's not herself, Paul. That's what we've just been saying."

"It's because of that dead body," said Paul promptly. "I have to admit I'm still kind of jumpy lately myself."

"If that's all it is, then what's the deal with the secrecy, the 'clean break'? Did you hear her say that stuff about the post office not giving out forwarding addresses? You'd think we were fugitives."

"What are you getting at?"

Ari fell into a chair. "I don't know. But something's wrong." She hesitated. "I wonder if it doesn't have something to do with our father."

Paul froze. "Why do you say that?"

"Because I feel as if he's close by." Ari's voice sank to a whisper. "Don't you?"

Paul glanced toward the door, as if he were afraid their mother might walk in and catch them talking. "What makes you think he's around here?"

Ari twirled a dark lock around her finger. "I don't know," she said. "It's a feeling I have. When I turn corners, I keep expecting him to be there. Does that make sense?"

"I bet it happens with lots of kids whose parents are divorced," said Paul. "It's maybe worse with us because Mom never talks about our dad. A kind of wish fulfillment, probably."

"Maybe you're right." It was hard for Ari to believe that Paul didn't share her feeling that their father was close by. "You honestly think it doesn't mean anything?" she asked.

Paul hesitated.

Ari stared at him a moment, then smiled. "You do have the same feeling, don't you? I knew it!"

"Maybe I do," he admitted. "But still it doesn't mean anything. Feelings aren't the same as facts."

"Yes," said Ari. "But if he were in town, it would explain why Mom was so nervous, wouldn't it?"

"I've got a lot of homework," Paul said, turning away from her abruptly. But Ari could see his pain.

CHAPTER THREE

THE VAMPIRE STEPPED OUT OF THE RAIN INTO A DIM and dusty shop near the French Market. The man behind the shop counter was round-shouldered with faded, thinning hair and gold-rimmed glasses the shape of half-moons. The glass display cases on which he rested his hands contained packets of tarot cards in different designs. On the shelves behind him were boxes of incense, joss sticks, clove cigarettes, and small wax dolls.

"May I help you?" inquired the shopkeeper.

"I would like a reading," said the vampire. Rain dripping from his cape made small puddles on the dusty floor. Drops of the rain had beaded on his soft, wide-brimmed hat.

"Have you had a reading here before?" asked the man.

"Yes," said the vampire.

"I'm sure I would remember," said the man,

peering curiously at the vampire's leprous white skin. "You have such an unusual face."

"It's been a long time since my last reading," the vampire said. He pushed through the cloth curtains that marked the entrance to the dark back room. It was little more than a closet situated directly behind the main part of the tiny shop. The vampire perched on one of the stools in front of the inclined board that stood, easel-like, at shoulder height. On it lay packs of tarot cards wrapped in soft cloths.

The shopkeeper shrugged and stepped into the reading room with him. He climbed onto the other stool and unwrapped a pack of cards. "Don't you want me to take your hat and coat?" he asked. "I can hang them up for you."

"No," said the vampire quickly. "I'm a little chilly. I . . . I haven't been well."

The shopkeeper smiled. "Nothing catching, I hope."

The vampire shook his head. "No. Nothing like that."

"Shuffle the cards," commanded the shopkeeper, handing the pack to him. "As you know, you must touch the cards."

Reluctantly, the vampire peeled off his gloves. In the dim light of the back room, his hands were a flash of white. He took half the deck in each hand and fanned them together so swiftly the cards were a blurred whir.

The shopkeeper giggled nervously. "You shuffle like a riverboat gambler." He paused. "Now, you must choose a card that can represent you."

The vampire chose a voluptuous woman in a gown spangled with stars.

The shopkeeper gazed at it a moment. "An unusual choice for a man," he commented.

"I'm an unusual man," said the vampire smoothly.

The shopkeeper laid the cards out on the board. For a moment he didn't speak. "Perhaps you'd like to reshuffle," he suggested, his voice expressionless. "There'll be no extra charge."

The vampire's cape rustled as he reached out to touch the shopkeeper's neck. His thin white hand rested there, and the man's glasses fell to the floor. Without them, his eyes looked watery and confused.

"Read the cards!" commanded the vampire.

"Someone whose life is closely entwined with yours will die today," said the shopkeeper.

The vampire embraced the man suddenly, and the stool he had been sitting on fell and tumbled against the cloth curtains, parting them slightly. He pressed his mouth against the man's neck and ripped the pulsing flesh with his teeth. The shopkeeper cried out, but the vampire covered his mouth until he was still. Then he sucked noisily, his face buried in the torn flesh until his nose and lips were smeared with blood. He let the body fall to the floor

"Fool!" he said contemptuously. He stepped over the man's body and carefully straightened the fallen stool so that the curtains hiding the back room swung closed once more. *Just in time,* he thought. A bell tinkled as the door to the shop opened.

"Anybody here?" called a voice.

"They've got tarot cards," said a different voice. "But I don't see anybody. The owner must be taking a coffee break."

He should have let the fool finish the reading, thought the vampire. But it was too late now for regrets. He pushed the back door of the shop open and slipped out to the alley behind the shop. Rain drummed noisily on the broken glass and pebbles that paved the alley. The vampire crouched on his haunches and peered into a muddy puddle at the rippled reflection of his face. *Handsome devil,* he thought, baring his white fangs in a smile. At least he had fed now, so he didn't look deathly pale. He scooped up the water in his cupped hands and splashed it on his face until the blood ran off his cheeks in pink rivulets.

His ears pricked at a thin shriek, and he lifted his head to glance at the back door of the shop. Someone had found the body already. He stood up abruptly, pulled his hat down over his eyes, and slipped away down the dark alley.

At school Ari stared out the tall window next to her desk. *This is what it must feel like to be lost at sea,* she told herself. *Lost and alone.* The glass was frosted with condensation inside, and rain ran in unending rivulets down the glass, melting the world outside into shapelessness. The teacher's voice droned on as Ari stared out the window. She wished she could tell Laurie that her mom was talking about moving out of town, but she was afraid to. What if her mother was in some kind of terrible trouble? She could have embezzled money or killed someone in a hit-and-run accident. Why else would she be so concerned about the post office giving out their new address? Ari gazed around the room. Half the class was asleep. She reminded herself that she mustn't let her imagination run away with her. Paul was always telling her that. It simply wasn't possible that their mother was on the run from the law—she was too honest. More likely she was trying to escape their father.

Ari knew that Paul longed to see their father, but even thinking about him frightened her. There must be some good reason their mother refused to talk about him, she figured. Perhaps he had made death threats against them all. Perhaps he was a drunk—or even an insane person. For all they knew, he was stalking them at this moment. Ari stared at the window, listening to her heart thump. She was definitely letting her imagination run away with her again.

Suddenly, a white face appeared at the rain-streaked window of the classroom. Dark eyes burned in the masklike face, blurred by the rain. Ari gasped and a whimper escaped her. The room around her grew dim.

Suddenly, a hand touched her shoulder. "Are you all right?" whispered Laurie.

Ari stared at her friend. "Look!" she cried. "The face at the window!" But when Laurie turned to look at the rain-streaked window, Ari noticed, the face was gone.

Mr. Burgess had given out graded tests, and kids were busy comparing answers.

"Someone was at the window," whispered Ari. "Look! His hand touched the glass."

The condensation on the window showed the clear print of a hand, as if something warm had touched the glass on the other side.

"An *A* for you as usual, Ari," said the teacher, tossing Ari's test on her desk.

But Ari continued to gaze at the handprint.

"No one is out there, Ari," Laurie told her. "You must have put your hand on the glass yourself."

"But I didn't," Ari whispered. She reached out to the cold glass and hesitantly fitted her hand into the handprint. The print was much larger than her hand. "Someone was out there," she said. "Someone is watching me."

"I think you've got this post-traumatic stress syndrome we studied in psychology," said Laurie. "Ever since Paul found that dead body, both of you have been on edge. That's the only reason you think somebody is watching you."

"No," said Ari. "Someone *is* watching me."

Laurie cleared her throat uncomfortably. Ari knew her friend didn't believe her.

When the twins got home from school, Ari could not shake a sense of uneasiness. She felt the stirring of old memories—of coming home from the playground at dusk and turning to see a dark figure standing in the shadows, his eyes glittering. "I'm sure someone was out there," she insisted to Paul. "Laurie didn't believe me, but someone was looking through the window."

"Maybe it was a janitor," suggested Paul.

"What would a janitor be doing outside in the pouring rain?"

Paul had no answer.

When darkness fell, the mist made a glowing halo around the streetlamp outside. The patter of the rain had stopped, but the cars outside made a noisy, whishing progress along the wet street.

"Mom's running late," said Paul. "Maybe we ought to go ahead and set the table and start dinner. She's going to be tired when she gets in."

Ari jumped up from her homework, thankful for the distraction of fixing dinner. But as soon as the twins got to the kitchen, the doorbell rang. "I'll get it," said Paul.

Ari was close behind him when he threw the door open. Two uniformed police officers were outside. One of them glanced at a card in his hand. "Is this Mary Ellen Montclair's house?" asked one of them.

"That's right," said Paul. "She's our mother. Can we help you?"

"Is your dad at home, kids?" asked the fat officer.

Ari glanced at Paul. "We don't have a dad. At least, he doesn't live here, and we don't even know where he is."

The older officer pushed his cap back on his head. "Maybe you should get your grandma to come over. Or your aunt or somebody."

"What is it?" asked Ari in a shrill birdlike voice she could hardly recognize as her own. "What's wrong?"

Paul put his arm around her. "We don't have any close relatives, Officer. Why don't you tell Ari and me what's going on?"

"I'm afraid your mother's been in an accident," said the fat officer.

"Is she in the hospital?" cried Ari. "We'd better go to her. Is she hurt? When did it happen?"

The officer shook his head. The pity in his eyes frightened Ari so much that she could not say any more.

"I'm sorry," he said. "They weren't able to save her."

"We have to go to her," sobbed Ari. "She'll be worried about us."

Paul squeezed her tight. "She's gone, Ari. That's what they're telling us. She's dead." He choked. "We have an aunt in Washington, D.C., Officer. I'll call her right away."

The two men looked relieved. "Do you have a friend you can stay with tonight?" the fat officer asked. "We can get a social worker to come pick you up, if you don't."

"I'll call the Bergers," said Paul. "They're friends of ours."

Paul was absolutely numb. It seemed that everything should stop in a freeze frame, yet cars continued to whoosh by on the treacherously wet streets outside. Paul could hear the static of the cops' radio in their patrol car. The shock was simply too much to comprehend. He dialed Mrs. Berger and told her what had happened. Then he found his mother's address book and called his father's sister, Aunt Gabrielle.

"Hello?" a male voice answered.

"Is Gabrielle there, please?" Paul asked. "This is her nephew, Paul."

"Sorry," the stranger's voice said. "Gabri's out jogging. May I take a message?"

"Tell her our mother has been killed in a car wreck. The police are here now, and they said we should call our next of kin."

"I'm so sorry! Of course, I'll tell Gabri as soon as she gets back."

Paul gave Aunt Gabrielle's friend the Bergers' number and hung up. His insides were an empty ache.

The policemen sat in the living room, impassive and still, while Paul and Ari packed.

Paul was in a daze as he threw some things in a duffel bag. He kept having the awful feeling that he could hear his mother's key turning in the lock. She would walk in any minute, as she had so many times before. *Better to get out of the house,* he thought, choking on his tears.

It seemed an eternity until Laurie's mother arrived. "You poor, poor lambs," Mrs. Berger cried, embracing them. "Laurie's still at the school play, but I came right over. You poor, poor babies." The police were obviously relieved to see an adult who could take charge of the twins.

Paul turned off the lights of the house as they left, then locked the door. When he glanced back at the dark, empty house, he felt a cold stab of pain. Nothing would ever be the same, he thought. All the life and warmth had bled from their house. It was an empty shell. Mrs. Berger shepherded them to her car. She blew her nose. "You poor, poor babies," she repeated brokenly.

"I've called our aunt," said Paul. "She wasn't in but I left a message for her. I gave her your phone number."

"I expect she'll take care of everything as soon as she gets here," said Mrs. Berger, looking relieved. "It's good you have a relative you can count on at a time like this."

Paul did not mention that he and Ari had never met their aunt. He already hated it that Mrs. Berger felt sorry for them. He dreaded seeing the pity in his friends' eyes even more. He glanced over at Ari. Her face was shiny and slick in the dim light of the car. As they sped through the quarter, her eyes brimmed, dark and gleaming with tears.

"Aunt Gabrielle will tell our father about what happened, Paul," Ari whispered to him. "He'll have to come for us now. He's all we've got."

Paul felt a sick clutch in his stomach. A horrible fear swept over him. Had he brought this disaster on them by wishing for his father to come?

*   *   *

36

The day of their mother's funeral was sunny. If only this bright interval had come a few days earlier, thought Ari bitterly, their mother would not have skidded on a rain-slicked street. The glare made her wince as she filed into the first row of folding chairs under a green canvas canopy. Their mother's shiny mahogany casket was before them, blanketed with fresh flowers. A crowd of friends filled the chairs under the canopy and spilled out onto the lawn of the cemetery. Ari recognized some of them—people from her mother's office, kids from school. They stood quietly on the dry, bleached grass, shifting their feet uncomfortably, looking stiff and formal in their best clothes.

Ari had cried most of the night, and her head ached. She knew she had to try not to think about her mother. She wished she could stop feeling altogether. If only she could blot everything out, she thought, and lose this pain! She was so desperate she might have stepped in front of a speeding car— but as soon as the thought formed in her mind, she knew that wouldn't be fair to Paul.

"Who's that?" Paul suddenly grabbed her arm.

Ari followed her twin's gaze and saw that he was looking at a tall, dark man who stood a bit apart from the crowd. The light glinted blankly on the man's sunglasses, robbing his face of expression.

"That's Mr. Cowgen, my calculus teacher," said Ari.

"Oh." Paul sighed his disappointment.

"Our father's not coming, Paul," said Ari harshly.

"He doesn't care about us. He never has." As soon as she said it, she felt better. It was as if her anger at her father burned away her grief. Ari watched the sick disappointment grow in Paul's eyes and knew that it mirrored the look on her own face.

Ari was sure Aunt Gabrielle had told their father about their mother's death—if anyone knew how to reach him, it would be his sister. At first, she and Paul had both felt certain they would hear from him, and for days they had jumped every time the Bergers' phone rang. They had stared at each other wide-eyed whenever the doorbell sounded. But there had been no word. No message. No phone call.

The twins had expected their aunt to come for the funeral, but a lawyer had contacted the Bergers instead and said that Aunt Gabrielle had been laid low by the flu. As her representative, he would take care of the funeral arrangements, he had said. Aunt Gabrielle planned to take the twins to live with her and she would come for them as soon as she was able to travel.

Paul looked over his shoulder at the crowd of well-wishers standing on the grass. He put his arm around Ari. "All we've got to do is get through this ceremony," he said softly. "Then it's got to get better."

Ari said nothing. Hot tears spilled out of her eyes. Paul pulled her close to him and they both sobbed.

*   *   *

The next day found the twins waiting for their aunt in the empty living room of the house on Rampart Street.

"I'm not sure I want to live in Washington, D.C.," said Ari nervously. "It's going to be awful going to a new school. I've seen the way people treat new kids."

"We have each other to talk to," Paul pointed out. "It could be worse."

"They'll probably make fun of our accents and our clothes. We won't have any friends at all."

"Trying to cheer us up?" said Paul with a crooked smile. "Look, it's going to be fine. We've got each other, don't we? We'll get along."

"I wish Aunt Gabrielle would show up." Ari shivered. Her voice echoed in the empty room. "She said she'd be here by eight. That was hours ago. And I wish the stupid lawyer hadn't had the electricity turned off so soon. And the phone. We're marooned here. We can't even call anybody."

She was glad Paul didn't point out that it had been her idea that they come back to Rampart Street to say good-bye to the old house. It had seemed like a good plan at the time, but Ari had not realized quite how unnerving it would be to wait in the empty place after dark. And she had not expected Aunt Gabrielle to be so late.

The streetlight outside cast an uncertain illumination through the bare front windows of the living room. It threw a glow on the uneasy faces of the twins, who sat on their suitcases. Shadows in the corners of the room seemed to move and grow.

A cloaked figure darted with swift, fluid movement up onto the porch, then tiptoed up to the door and peered through the window at the twins. Shadowed by a broad-brimmed hat, violet eyes glowed in the dark like radioactive jewels. An abundance of hair fell to the shoulders of the cape, which shimmered, intensely black, in the lamp-light. A skeletally thin hand was lifted; its white fingers with pink oval nails nervously crept up the window frame, and tiny phosphorescent dots glowed where each fingertip touched.

CHAPTER
FOUR

ARI GLANCED AT THE WINDOW, TROUBLED BY THE
feeling she was being watched, but no one was
there. "What'll we do if she doesn't show up?" she
asked suddenly.

"We could probably stay with the Bergers for a
little while longer," said Paul. "I guess."

Ari did not see how Paul could sleep on the
Bergers' couch indefinitely. And it wasn't as if they
had been invited. "I wonder if orphanages still
exist," she said in a small voice.

"She's going to show up," said Paul. "She's late,
that's all."

"What's that?" Anne-Marie cried suddenly.

Paul glanced at the window. "Nothing," he said.
"Calm down."

Ari hugged herself and shivered. A signature
on a card, a disembodied flutey voice—Aunt
Gabrielle seemed so insubstantial. If only they

knew her, she thought, maybe they wouldn't feel so nervous.

Ari wished she had a flashlight, but the flashlight had been packed along with all the other household goods. Her flesh crawled with self-consciousness. She was sure she could feel a stranger's eyes on her. She stood up abruptly. "I can't stand this anymore. I think we ought to wait over at Mr. Wilson's house. We can leave a note for Aunt Gabrielle."

A rapid knock sounded on the door, and the twins started.

"Darlings! It's Auntie Gabrielle!" trilled a richly musical voice.

Paul jumped up and threw the door open. He was greeted by a cape swishing through the air and white extended arms. At first, crushed close to his aunt's breast, he had only an impression of a large hat, sparkling violet-colored eyes, and a stifling expensive scent. "Dearest, dearest," she murmured, her breath tickling his ear. He didn't know what to say to her and was relieved when she turned to Ari. "Ari, dearest!"

Paul's gaze fell to his aunt's small, tightly laced boots. They looked like the sort of shoes a witch might wear, he thought. But when Aunt Gabrielle turned toward him again, he could see that she was a fashionably dressed woman in a long camel-colored skirt and a cashmere sweater. She was so thin he could see the points of her hipbone under the soft material of the skirt. Her cheekbones were broad and in the uncertain light almost seemed to cast shadows. Gold bracelets glimmered at one bony wrist. Her eyes glowed at him—violet and hypnotic like a cat's. Meeting her gaze, Paul had the odd sensation that he was falling, tumbling into something deep. Her cheerful voice startled him back to consciousness. "Darlings, it's dreadful we have to rush like this, but we literally don't have a minute to waste. Our tickets are on the next flight out!" she cried. "If only my beastly plane hadn't been so late."

"No problem," said Paul. "Ari and I are all packed." He hoisted the suitcases.

After they stepped out, Paul carefully locked the door of the house even though there was nothing left inside. Then he tossed the suitcases into the trunk of Aunt Gabrielle's shiny rental car.

"Allons, mes enfants!" Aunt Gabrielle cried as she got in behind the wheel. "Let's get a move on!"

"I think she wears contact lenses," hissed Ari, "and they're tinted. That's what gives them that strange violet color."

The twins got into the backseat of the car. Aunt Gabrielle plucked a long hat pin from her crown and set her big hat on the seat beside her. "Gracious, it's warm down here," she said. "I hope you packed sweaters. It's cooler in Washington, and the movers won't be arriving with the rest of your things for a few days."

The twins assured her that they had packed warm clothes. The streets of the French Quarter whizzed by the car windows. Old-fashioned street-lamps cast a glow on gently decaying old town houses with lacy black balconies. Plastic garbage bags bulged by the curb. Perhaps this was the last time they would be gazing on the streets of their hometown and smelling the familiar smells of gumbo, filé, and garbage, thought Ari. The shiny car passed college kids in T-shirts, silver-haired tourists from the Midwest, thin punk couples with spiked hair. Ari could feel her throat filling up with tears. She realized she would miss the tourists. The house on Rampart Street was empty now and was to be sold. Would they ever come home again?

"Everywhere I look there are T-shirt shops," complained Aunt Gabrielle, peering ahead. "Can't something be done before they take over the entire Quarter?"

"I think somebody's formed an association," said Paul. "I saw a T-shirt about it the other day."

Ari laughed suddenly and covered her mouth, embarrassed by the explosive sound.

"Did you have any trouble finding our house?" asked Paul.

His aunt's smile flashed in the rearview mirror. "Not a bit. Your directions were wonderful, darling. And I do know my way around here a little. I spent a summer in New Orleans once many years ago."

The twins exchanged a look. Aunt Gabrielle had once lived in New Orleans? Had it been perhaps the summer their parents had met?

The rented car sped past the dark shores of Lake Pontchartrain with its silent fishermen standing on the banks. They drove past dark bayous, the ancient riverbeds of the Mississippi. Overhead planes droned. Paul peered out the window and saw one coming in low, its red lights glowing.

The rented Lincoln pulled up at the brightly lit terminal, and Paul opened his door and got out. A luggage cart squeaked by, narrowly missing him. Aunt Gabrielle unlocked the trunk. "You go on in, darlings. There's no need for you to return the rental car with me. Go on to the gate and I'll catch up with you." She climbed back into the car.

As she drove off, the twins stood together on the sidewalk and silently watched the shiny Lincoln disappear. "She's very pretty." Ari turned to her twin. "Do you think she looks like our dad?"

Paul shrugged. "Maybe." The crushing disappointment of not having his father even show up for the funeral had left a painful emptiness aching inside of him. The twins moved toward the terminal and the automatic doors swung open.

The air-conditioning of the terminal hit them like a blast, and Ari tightened her grip on her suitcase. "It's very possible that after the split Mom didn't want to have anything to do with Dad's family. Maybe that's why Aunt Gabrielle never came to see us."

"You mean, just because she's Dad's sister?" asked Paul.

"Well, it's not like our parents had one of those friendly divorces," said Ari.

The terminal was packed with passengers carrying tote bags slung over one shoulder or pulling suitcases behind them on wheels. Indian families in saris, college students in sweat suits, business-women in gray flannel moved purposefully down the broad corridor.

At gate ten, the first-class passengers were already lined up to board. Aunt Gabrielle swept up suddenly, her cape flying. "That's us, *mes cheris.* We'd better get in line."

"We're flying first class?" Ari stared in astonishment

Aunt Gabrielle nodded. She was groping in her pocketbook for the tickets. The twins got into line at once. "She must be rich if we're flying first class," said Ari in a low voice.

The twins had gone with their mother to California on vacation the year before, and Paul had learned then that he was too tall to fit comfortably into a regular coach seat. The seats in first class were much roomier, Paul discovered. Stretching out, he decided he could easily get used to being rich.

Aunt Gabrielle settled into the aisle seat and beamed at him. "There, isn't this nice? I was able to get us three seats together so we can chat."

Coach passengers were filing in now. Nearby two men talked rapidly in German. Somewhere a baby cried.

At last the "FASTEN SEAT BELT" sign flashed on, and the plane began to hum and vibrate.

Aunt Gabrielle leaned over Paul and said, "I'm so sorry I couldn't make it down for your mother's funeral." She smiled wryly. "That wretched flu.

And at the worst possible time." She patted Paul on the knee. "But now we're going to get to know each other and make up for all those lost years, aren't we?" Paul felt his ears pop and forced himself to yawn. The stewardess appeared with a beverage cart, and to his astonishment she offered them glasses of champagne. He supposed the laws on underage drinking didn't apply on planes.

"The bubbles tickle," complained Ari. She downed her glass at once. "I'll have another, please," she said to the stewardess. Smiling, the stewardess refilled her glass.

Paul had never tasted champagne. He didn't like it and decided to down it quickly as Ari had. The stewardess instantly refilled his glass.

"The second glass tastes better than the first," Ari confided, looking at him owlishly.

But after the second glass, Paul's head felt too large, and the seat in front of him seemed to swell and recede. The boundaries of the plane were vague, as if he were flying through the air in a phantom jet. The reflection of Ari's face in the dark oval of the window hinted at the presence of spirits outside in the blackness.

"Darlings, you're going to simply adore Washington!" Aunt Gabrielle's voice seemed to come from far away.

"I'm not so sure," said Paul. His voice sounded too loud to his ears. "My friend David used to live in Washington when his dad was an aide for Senator Nussbaum, and he hated it. He said the place is full of bloodsuckers."

Aunt Gabrielle's hand jerked suddenly, and her glass tipped over. A spray of droplets glimmered on the cashmere sweater like tiny jewels. Her smile was rigid as she righted the glass quickly, then grabbed a paper cocktail napkin and blotted her sweater. "Stupid of me," she said.

"Anyway," Paul went on, "David hated it."

Aunt Gabrielle gave a throaty laugh. "But of course, my dear, your life won't be like your friend's. You'll move in quite different circles." She squeezed his knee. "I know it's a wrench for you, dear, leaving your home, but I hope you'll learn to love your new home as much as you did your old one."

Paul must have fallen asleep after that, because all of a sudden he felt the plane touch down with a bump and his eyes flew open. The seat belt signs were on, but already he could hear shuffling in the aisles and the thud of carry-on luggage being pulled down from overhead compartments. His head ached.

Ari rubbed a circle on the frosted window. "It's raining outside." She sniffled. Her dark hair was tousled, and her cheeks were flushed from sleep.

Paul felt drugged as they made their way off the plane. He wasn't wearing a watch, but he knew it must be the small hours of the morning. Not that he could have guessed it by looking around the terminal. The fluorescent lights were harsh, and the uniformed airport employees hurried about with brisk energy. Only the waiting passengers slumped exhausted in their plastic seats, like bags of laundry.

Aunt Gabrielle pinned her hat to her hair. "There's no sense in all of us getting wet," she said. "I'll get the car and pick you up in front." Her dainty black boots clicked on the marble flooring as she walked away. The twins watched as the big glass doors swung open and their aunt's cloaked figure became vague and insubstantial in the gray half-light. Then she disappeared into blackness.

"Does it seem to you Aunt Gabrielle is kind of strange?" asked Ari.

"Everything seems strange to me all of a sudden," said Paul, shaking his head. "I wish I hadn't drunk that champagne."

"She must be a lot younger than our father," said Ari. "I mean, I figure Dad must be about forty, like Mom was. Aunt Gabrielle doesn't look forty."

"She doesn't look like a kid either, though," Paul suggested. His gaze rested on his twin with satisfaction. The gold hoops in Ari's ears made glimmers of light where they peeked through her dark hair.

"Aunt Gabrielle doesn't look any particular age at all," Ari said, puzzled. "Not old. Not young exactly, either."

"She looks good, though," suggested Paul. In fact, something about her reminded him of Ari.

A car horn blew outside the door. "That's her," cried Ari. "She's here."

"Ari." Paul gave his twin a stern look. "Listen, don't start imagining things. You know how you get carried away sometimes. Aunt Gabrielle's being really nice to us, and we don't want to do anything that might hurt her feelings."

Aunt Gabrielle's black Mercedes hummed at the curb. Paul heaved the suitcases in, the doors slammed, the car's big engine roared, and they were off. The wet roadway gleamed under their wheels, and the car's windshield wipers clacked monotonously.

Paul had the sense that vast black skies stretched overhead. Even in the dark, Washington seemed more open than New Orleans.

"Do you think you'll be up to going to school this first day?" Aunt Gabrielle smiled over her shoulder. "Or do you want to sleep in?"

"Might as well get started," said Ari.

Paul glanced at her in surprise. He knew that she was dreading going to the new school.

"Well, you probably should start as soon as possible," agreed Aunt Gabrielle, "if you think you're up to it. The course work moves very quickly, and you don't want to get behind. St. Anselm's is one of the best schools in Washington." She looked smug. "It has everything—a marvelous library, a theater, lovely playing fields. It's a favorite with the children of diplomats and high government officials."

Ari's heart sank. Already she could imagine the freezing looks she would get from the snobby kids at St. Anselm's. She longed for the familiar run-down brick school building in New Orleans.

"It's very tough to get in," said Aunt Gabrielle, "but I was able to pull a few strings for you.

Luckily, there are still some places in Washington where family connections count."

The car made a soft drumming noise as it crossed the seams in the cement bridge over the Potomac River. On either side of them stood rose-white government buildings. Looming ahead and then filling up the sky was the huge, floodlit Washington Monument. The circlet of American flags planted around it in the grass flapped in the rainy wind. Brightly lit streets, shiny in the rain, whizzed by Paul's window.

"My housekeeper, Carmel, is coming in the morning," Aunt Gabrielle went on, "so she can drive you to school. I still have some work to do tonight, so I'll be sleeping late."

The black car glided up in front of an elegant brick town house. Its shiny front door gleamed in the lamplight. "Home, sweet home!" Aunt Gabrielle cried.

Aunt Gabrielle pressed a black disk in her hand, and a green garage door to the left of the house slowly lifted. "Like magic, isn't it?" said Aunt Gabrielle with a strange little smile.

The garage was cold and dimly lit. Shivering, the twins unloaded their suitcases and followed their aunt out a side door and down a narrow path that ran between the house and the garage. Something scuttled in the dead leaves that littered the pathway, and Paul felt his flesh creep.

Aunt Gabrielle pushed open a tall gate and stepped out onto the sidewalk. Paul could see then that the entire street was lined with town houses.

To eyes accustomed to the funky charm of the French Quarter, the street looked too neat. Paul wasn't sure he liked the polished and citified look, all the glossy front doors and tidy brick. Nearby a tree's leaves shivered in the breeze.

"I feel like a zombie," Paul said thickly.

Aunt Gabrielle shot him a startled look as she pushed the front door open. "What did you say, dear?"

"I've got to get some sleep," said Paul. "Aren't you tired, Aunt Gabrielle? I'm dead on my feet."

She smiled at him. "I'm a night owl, I'm afraid." Paul heard a click and light flooded the long hallway. A black-and-white checkerboard floor stretched out before them. An umbrella stand was by the door next to a small table with an odd black statuette of a rooster. To their left, stairs rose into darkness.

"If you're tired," said Aunt Gabrielle, "we'll go right upstairs and get you to bed." She switched on the light on the staircase.

A step creaked under Paul's foot as they mounted the stairway.

A strip of blood-colored carpet ran the length of the windowless upstairs hall. Ari was vaguely conscious of mirrors, of odd pieces of tall black furniture and the stuffed body of a crow sitting on a small table, its black eyes glinting malignantly. When they were halfway down the hall, Ari turned back to give the bird a second look, halfway expecting to catch it moving. Its image was doubled

52

by a narrow black mirror that hung behind it. Again she had that feeling that she was being watched. But the crow had not moved, and as Ari looked at it she realized that its feathers had been dulled by a film of dust.

Aunt Gabrielle stepped to the end of the hallway and pushed open a door. "Here is your room, Paul." She turned on the bedside lamp, and the room was flooded with spooky shadows. "I had Carmel make up the bed for you so you can turn right in. And look at this!" She flung open a door. It opened onto another bedroom. "Ari has the room right next to yours. This little door goes between them. Isn't that nice?"

Ari felt a thud of relief that Paul was going to be close at hand. They would be able to talk to each other privately without going out into the creepy hallway.

Aunt Gabrielle clasped her hands and regarded the twins, dewy-eyed. "I knew you'd want to be close," she cried. "I remember how close your dear father and I were at your age. We were absolutely inseparable!"

"Where is our father living these days?" asked Paul. Ari turned to him, her mouth open in shock.

Aunt Gabrielle had frozen a half-instant in midgesture. But like a film when the projector is turned on again, she quickly went on as if nothing had happened. "Oh, here, there, everywhere," she cried gaily. "Richard's quite the rolling stone. I never know where he's going to turn up next." She beamed at the twins. "Well, sleep tight, dear ones." She pecked Paul and Ari on their cheeks. Her lips were startlingly cold. "It's going to be simply delightful having you here. I'm so very happy!"

After the bedroom door closed, they heard her boot heels tap outside, then silence.

Ari felt miserable. The dark shadows of the old house were full of menace, and the thumping of her heart shook her. With all her heart she wished for their comfortable house in New Orleans. The loss of her mother was suddenly very real. Sobbing, she flung her arms around Paul. "Don't leave me!" she cried.

Paul stroked her hair. "I'm not going anyplace, Ari. I'll be right next door."

"Let's leave the connecting door open," said Ari.

"Hey, no problem," said Paul.

As he opened his suitcase and got ready for bed, Paul could hear Ari moving around in the next room. The sound was vaguely comforting. Even when Ari was getting all wrought up, her presence steadied him. It was as if she were being nervous for both of them. He could be calm while she was freaking out. It went the other way, too. He didn't fall apart as often as she did, but when he did—that time he had to get stitches at the hospital and there was blood all over the place, for instance—Ari was a rock. He wondered how people managed when they didn't have a twin.

He was exhausted but he had never felt less sleepy in his life. His jaw was clenched and he felt nerves jumping around under his skin.

"Paul?" came Ari's plaintive voice.

He sighed with relief and stepped into her room. A tree just outside her window cast a moving shadow on the wall, and crystal pendants hanging from the bedside lamp moved and glittered as if stirred by an unseen hand. Ari's face above the counterpane was a pale smudge in the darkness. "You're too far away!" she said in a small voice.

"Move over," he said. "I'll get in with you."

The bed was an old-fashioned three-quarter-sized bed, so it was a bit crowded with both of them. But that was okay. He needed the comfort of her warmth next to him and the sound of her breathing. It reminded him of when they were small and their mother used to put them down together to nap. Almost at once, he fell asleep.

CHAPTER
FIVE

THE NEXT MORNING, RAIN RATTLED AGAINST THE TALL panes of the window, and only a thin gray light leaked in. Ari could see the tall bureau and the fireplace, but brighter and more real than the furniture were the fanged creatures in the room. Their noses were blunt and their nostrils flared. Their ears were broad and pointed. They crouched beside the bed, domestic and unremarkable as cats, sitting on their hairy haunches, examining their front claws as if they were considering a manicure. A small one was peering in her suitcase. She could see his naked haunches, pink and sparsely haired. He tottered and almost lost his balance in his curiosity.

Don't touch my things! Ari wanted to scream. But she couldn't scream—the sound wouldn't come out. The creature by her bed smiled and she saw his fangs clearly. "No!" she cried aloud. At once the creatures were gone, vanished like smoke in the wind. Ari propped herself up on her elbows and looked around. It had only been a dream. She was breathing hard. *They can't hurt me,* she assured herself. *They aren't real.* But she still felt strange, different somehow—as if something had changed. Then she remembered. Their mother was dead and they were living with Aunt Gabrielle.

Paul was breathing evenly, half-asleep. For an instant, Ari was tempted to wake him and tell him about the fanged creatures, but she was afraid to. What if they were a sign she was cracking up? She had never told Paul that she saw numbers and letters in color, either. She didn't like to think about it. It meant that she was seriously different. Different even from her twin.

"Ari?" Paul asked fuzzily. "You awake?"

"Yes, I'm awake," she said.

Paul swung his legs around over the side of the bed. "We'd better get moving. Look at the clock. It's already seven."

"I bet we don't have to be there on time the first day," said Ari, but she slid out of bed.

When the twins went downstairs, they found that a woman with her hair in a heavy dark braid was putting a silver-domed dish on the dining room table. The velvet curtains of the dining room were drawn tight against the gloom outside, and a large chandelier with hundreds of crystal prisms glittered over the table.

They heard Aunt Gabrielle's footsteps on the

marble floor of the hallway. Then she came in. Her face was deathly pale and her violet eyes were cast in shadow by the swirl of abundant black hair that fell partly over her face and rested on her shoulders. Her tight houndstooth jacket, cinched in to show her tiny waist, had double-breasted black buttons that matched her pencil-thin skirt.

"I don't want to trouble Carmel to drive you to school, after all," Aunt Gabrielle said. "I'll take you myself this morning. Of course, what we'll have to do as soon as possible is get you a car."

Paul wondered if Aunt Gabrielle had a spare Mercedes somewhere that she wasn't using. He certainly wouldn't mind driving one to school.

Carmel lifted the silver cover to reveal a steaming platter of eggs and bacon. "The usual school day starts at eight o'clock." Aunt Gabrielle tapped absentmindedly on the snowy tablecloth with a pink-enameled fingernail, then glanced at her watch. She smiled at the twins. "But don't rush with your breakfast."

Paul and Ari glanced at each other uneasily, then proceeded to bolt their food.

It was raining when the twins got to school. The windshield wipers swished with nerve-racking monotony as Aunt Gabrielle's Mercedes pulled up in the circular drive.

Misty rain swirled around the car when they got out. Ari and Paul were buffeted by the wind, and they struggled to keep a single umbrella over their heads. The wind lifted Aunt Gabrielle's plaid rain cape and forced her to keep one hand on top of her saucer-shaped hat. "Your father went to school here," said Aunt Gabrielle, raising her voice to be heard over the wind. "Of course, that was years ago, before the school went coed."

Ari stooped a bit to see out from under the umbrella. The foul weather made a kind of twilight into which the lighted windows of the school's buildings glowed, hinting at warmth and comfort within. The buildings, made of irregular stones and bricks, had windows like those in a church, pointed at the top and divided into many small glowing panes.

Looking around at the damp and plushy greenness of the gently rolling lawns and the splash of golden leaves overhead, Ari had a sudden strong sense that she belonged here—something inside her slid into place with an almost perceptible click. She had expected to feel overwhelmed; instead, she felt a pleasurable excitement, as if the curtain were about to go up and she was the star of the play.

Suddenly a boy rocketed around a corner and collided with them. The umbrella landed upside down in the muddy gutter. The boy bent over and hastily peeled his wet papers off of the sidewalk. When he straightened up, droplets of water glistened on his nose. He was almost eye to eye with Ari. "Wow!" he breathed. For a moment he stared at her in stunned silence.

"Nobody hurt?" cried Aunt Gabrielle. "I hope your papers didn't get too wet."

"I'm okay. No bones broken. I'd hang around a while and propose marriage," the boy said, looking at Ari, "but I think I'd better go get a towel or something first."

Ari laughed shyly.

"Try coming on strong," muttered Paul.

The boy was wearing a blazer and a tie that was half undone and dangled loosely around his neck. He might have conformed to the dress code, but he nevertheless managed to look disreputable. His wet hair was plastered onto his face and his smile was dazzling.

"Let's get out of this rain, children!" urged Aunt Gabrielle. "We're all getting soaked."

Paul retrieved the umbrella, shook it, then pulled Ari close next to him. He trudged after Aunt Gabrielle, who seemed at least to know where she was going. Rain leaked into his shoes and made his socks soggy. He saw Ari glance over her shoulder and he couldn't stop himself from looking back, too.

The boy they had run into was standing in the rain, watching them with a goofy smile on his face. "Jeez," muttered Paul. "Give me a break."

"I like this place," said Ari.

The Schuler Building—its name was cut into the stone archway over the entrance—had wide glass doors. They pushed the doors open and stepped in out of the rain. The headmaster's office, a corner room, was full of windows, but the day was so dark not even walls of windows could dispel the gloom. The bookshelves were tightly packed with well-used books. Paul sank into a chair. He wished he could take off his wet socks and put his head under a dryer.

The headmaster wrung Aunt Gabrielle's hand. "So glad you could make it, after all, Gabri. And these are our new scholars, eh?"

The headmaster and Aunt Gabrielle were old pals, it turned out. They had served together on a panel discussion about Romania. They fell to talking about people they both knew. Someone named Taki had gotten in trouble with the government and some senator—Paul didn't catch the name—was threatening to publish his racy and revealing diaries. "Blackmail," said Aunt Gabrielle, shaking her head.

"He must be desperate," said the headmaster.

Paul sat, feeling a bit left out of things, wondering where he fit in. Aunt Gabrielle and the headmaster were obviously lost in mutual admiration.

Ari caught a glimpse of the expression on her twin's face and wanted to put her arms around him and reassure him, but she felt an unfamiliar sense of constraint. Hugging each other was okay back at their old school where everyone had known them since first grade. But here, among strangers, she was afraid people would think it was odd.

Ari was in a more advanced math class than Paul, so they had different class schedules. During first-period calculus, Ari sensed she was the center of attention and felt nervous and excited. It was turning out to be more interesting than she had thought to be the new girl. But she missed her twin, and to make it worse, when she caught a brief glimpse of Paul in the hall, he looked confused. His unhappiness tugged at her, spoiling her pleasure in the new school.

But her spirits lifted when she saw the boy she had run into that morning standing outside the library. Ari noticed that a petite, dark girl was looking up at him, her hand resting confidingly on his chest while he frowned down at her unhappily. Neither of them noticed Ari as she passed, but she was acutely conscious of their presence as if they'd been outlined in neon. *The pretty girl must be his girlfriend,* Ari figured. If that was the way it was, she hoped the relationship was on the skids. *Interesting possibilities there,* she thought, and as she moved to her next class, she smiled to herself. Maybe something good was going to happen with that boy who had smiled at her so dazzlingly that morning.

Later in the morning, she bumped into her twin on a staircase, and she caught her breath sharply in sudden relief. She hated knowing that she would be in different classes from Paul all day. It made her feel unplugged.

"Where are you going?" Paul asked.

"I don't know," Ari said. "I'm lost."

Paul laughed. "Me, too."

"Are you okay, Paul?" She searched his face anxiously.

He smiled. "Sure. You know it takes me longer to get to know people than it does you. I'm just

62

feeling a little out of it. I'll get over it. Don't let me rain on your parade. I can tell you're feeling at home already."

"I like it here," she admitted. "It's funny. I was so worried about fitting in, but as soon as we got here I felt right away that I belonged." She glanced up at the narrow stained-glass window that gave the staircase its only light. "I don't know why exactly." She shot Paul an anxious look. She wanted him to like it, too.

"One thing's the same, anyway," Paul said. "We've still got each other."

At lunch, the students sat at round tables, each with an oversized bottle of apple juice—and a teacher. There was little noise and confusion. This, obviously, was not a school where food fights were routine. Ari's history teacher sat near her. He was a young-looking man with a beard who seemed more interested in the food than in conversation. Ari looked around the long, noisy dining room they called the refectory. Stained-glass panes were inset into the top of long, pointed windows, and the walls were wood paneled. The place had the look of a dining room in a medieval castle. Ari kept an eye out for the boy she had run into, but so far no luck. The girl next to her was a skinny girl with braces and high, arched eyebrows that gave her a perpetually surprised look. "I'm Sybil," she said. "You're new, huh? You're already in calculus? Is that a mix-up in your schedule or are you some kind of genius?"

Ari shrugged. "I like math."

"So who was that guy you checked in with this morning?"

"My brother, Paul."

"Are you French?" asked Sybil. Ari pronounced Paul's name in the French way, "pole" instead of "pawl."

Ari frowned. "No. Well, not exactly. A lot of people in our family have French names. I'm not sure why."

"Where are you from?"

"New Orleans."

"Oh, well, that explains it. Cajun."

The French names came from her father's side of the family, and as far as Ari could make out her father's family wasn't from New Orleans—but she didn't want to get into that.

Sybil lifted a forkful of turkey and dressing. "So your brother's in the fourth form?"

Ari looked blank.

"That's the tenth grade," the girl explained. "I'm sorry. I know it takes a while to catch on to the lingo around here."

"No, he's a junior." Ari smiled. "I mean he's in the fifth form, same as me. We're twins."

"Oh? Identical?" Sybil blushed. "Stupid of me. Of course, you can't be identical. You're a boy and he's a girl. I mean, he's a boy and you're a girl."

Ari grinned. "If you're being friendly just to get to know my brother, Sybil, I'm going to be *so* disappointed."

"I'm not." Sybil's face was pink. "I only happened to notice him, that's all. May I be brutally frank?"

Ari blinked. She hated it when people were brutally frank. They always seemed determined to tell you that your hairstyle didn't become you or that your character was full of flaws. "Sure," she said hesitantly. "Shoot."

"My best friend just moved away. Her dad got a posting in Japan. So I am now interviewing possible replacements."

"Fair enough," said Ari equably. "I myself am new in school and looking for transitional people that I can hang around with until I find some real friends."

"Jeez!" Sybil stared at her. "Talk about brutally frank!"

Suddenly both girls burst into laughter.

Paul heard Ari's laughter when he came into the refectory. He glanced over at her and brightened. She was sitting next to a skinny girl with a frizzy mane of red-gold hair. As soon as he got his food, he went over and squeezed a chair in between them. Ari introduced him to Sybil with a self-conscious glance and Sybil turned pink. It didn't take a mind reader to figure out that Sybil found Paul attractive.

"If you weren't some kind of math whiz, Ari," he mumbled, "we might have some classes together. You having calculus throws our schedules out of sync."

"Sorry about that." Ari smiled. "Sybil here says

she noticed us when we checked in this morning."

"Stands to reason that anybody would notice Aunt Gabrielle," said Paul.

"The lady in the cape?" Sybil straightened suddenly. "The one getting into the Mercedes?"

"That's her. That's our aunt," said Ari. "We're living with her now since our mother died."

Sybil paled. "Oh, I'm so sorry!"

An awkward silence fell.

"I think I'm going to like it here," said Ari, determinedly changing the subject. "This looks like a nice school. An interesting place."

Sybil glanced around the room. "It looks a lot more diverse than it is. If you struck out everybody whose parents didn't work with some government or another, the place would be practically empty. Maybe just me and Jack Montgomery."

"Seriously?" asked Ari.

"I may exaggerate some," admitted Sybil. "I usually do. I guess a lot of people's parents are doctors or lawyers or something. And some of them are from Pongo Pongo or someplace where the government isn't really a government. Not the way we think of it, anyway. What does your aunt do?"

"She teaches night classes at the foreign policy school of Johns Hopkins," said Paul.

"Spook!" Sybil whooped, then hastily covered her mouth with her hand. "Sorry."

"W-what do you mean?" asked Ari, darting an anxious glance at Paul.

Sybil blushed. "I mean that sounds like a CIA

front job. All the people who work for the CIA have jobs like that. Did I mention that we have some CIA kids and a kid whose dad was ex-KGB, too?" She glanced first at one twin and then the other. "Not that I mean your aunt is really CIA," she said hastily. "It stands to reason that some perfectly legitimate people must work at these jobs, right? I didn't mean anything."

"I don't think she's CIA," said Paul shortly.

The twins were silent for a moment, taken aback by Sybil's remark. "Spook" was slang for "spy," but it reminded them powerfully of Aunt Gabrielle. Something about her was uncomfortably spooky.

Paul glanced around the table at the other kids, all of whom were talking animatedly and ignoring him. He was going to have to join the track team or something, he thought. It would be a way to get to know people.

Just then Paul saw the boy who had run into Ari that morning. Paul hoped the guy would not notice them. No such luck. He came right over to their table.

"You're late for lunch, Cos," said Mr. Fleming. "A creative excuse, as usual? Come on, you must have one. Don't disappoint us."

"The cat ate my gym shoes," said Cos, glancing at Ari.

Mr. Fleming's beard twitched. "That one's been overused. Not one of your better efforts."

"Actually," Cos admitted, "I left my book bag at

67

the activities building and I had to go get it."

"Boring but probably true," said Mr. Fleming. "You'd better get something to eat before it's all gone. You may be irritating, but we don't want you to starve to death."

"Who's that?" Ari whispered to Sybil.

"Cos Cosgrove," Sybil whispered back. "But don't get your hopes up. He's already taken. He goes with Nadia Tanasescu."

"Nadia? Is she a tiny little girl, very pretty?" Ari remembered the girl she had seen Cos with that morning.

"That's her," said Sybil.

Suddenly Ari longed for the confusion of her old cafeteria. She had never realized before how its chaos had offered a certain privacy. At these circular tables with a teacher at each one, she felt she had to be careful what she said.

"Mr. Fleming," Sybil piped up, "Ari and I have already finished. May we go?"

Mr. Fleming eyed their plates dubiously, but he nodded.

"Let's go to the commons, where we can talk," hissed Sybil. The hallway outside the refectory was lined with book bags that students had tossed to the floor when they went in to eat. Stepping over them, Sybil led Ari to the commons room. A broad archway separated the commons room from the hallway. It was a brightly lit room with a grouping of comfortable chairs in front of a fireplace. The walls were decorated with photographs of long-ago sports teams. A brightly colored heraldic shield hung over the mantel. Sybil hurled herself into a leather chair. "So, do you like Cos?" she asked breathlessly.

Ari was a bit taken aback, but she laughed.

"He's absolutely Nadia's greatest coup," Sybil went on. "Nobody noticed her until Cos did."

"How long have they been going together?"

Sybil frowned. "I'm not sure. It must have happened over the summer, because I remember on the first day he was sort of hanging around her and she was looking really happy, like a lightbulb was turned on inside her. He used to say he didn't want to go with somebody who went to school here, but I guess that was before he fell for Nadia. He always used to go with somebody he met at camp or at a math competition or something. You know, somebody he didn't have to see every day."

"So, what's Nadia really like once you get to know her?"

"Who gets to know her?" Sybil shrugged. "I don't know. I guess she's very sweet. Her family's from Romania."

Aunt Gabrielle and the headmaster had been talking about Romania that morning, thought Ari. It seemed she was bumping into Romania everywhere. She would have to check it out on a map.

"Where is that?" she asked Sybil.

Sybil shrugged. "Central Europe somewhere. You've heard of it. The mountainous part of it used to be called Transylvania."

Ari had heard of Transylvania, all right. That

was where the vampires in movies came from.

"Look, Ari," said Sybil, "I'm not sure going after Cos is a good idea. Not that I want to discourage you or anything, but I think when you're new at school it's better to sort of ease in carefully."

Ari thought of Cos's dazzling smile. "Maybe Nadia and Cos aren't getting along very well. Maybe Cos is looking around for somebody else."

"Wishful thinking?" asked Sybil, raising her eyebrows. "If he breaks up with her, Nadia will crack up. She adores him. And Amanda will hate you for it." She cringed. "Jeez, speak of the devil. Here she comes."

A girl with a determined look suddenly walked by them. She was flushed with color, and her ruffled cap of hair brushed against a firm jaw.

"That's Amanda," whispered Sybil. "She's Nadia's best friend."

Ari gazed after the girl. "She sure looks different from Nadia. Nadia looks so meek."

"You're right," Sybil agreed at once. "They're completely different. Amanda tells dirty jokes, gets carried away when she dances, and doesn't ever get embarrassed. Honestly, Amanda might do *anything*. Kelly Griswold was in second grade with her at some Quaker school, and she said Amanda glued the class turtle to the turtle bowl." Sybil paused. "So anyway, tell me about Paul."

"Paul?" Ari looked blank.

"Your brother, remember? If you can make yourself stop thinking about Cos for just a minute, I'd like to hear what your brother is like."

"Paul?" Ari shrugged. "I don't know. I guess he's a lot like me."

"Does he have a girlfriend back in New Orleans?" Sybil asked.

Ari shook her head.

"What sort of girl does he like, do you think?"

"Empty-headed and sexy," said Ari promptly. No sense letting Sybil get her hopes up. "He hasn't actually had a serious girlfriend yet, but from what I've seen so far he has rotten taste."

"How can you say he's like you, then?" asked Sybil. "Well, I kind of like sexy types myself," Ari admitted.

"Sexy is a relative term," said Sybil stoutly. "Everybody is sexy to somebody. It's a personal and mysterious quality."

"Not true! What about Mr. Fleming, the history teacher? Beards are definitely not sexy," protested Ari.

"That's different," said Sybil.

Ari grinned. "Whenever people know you're right they always say, 'That's different.'"

"You may be a teensy bit right," admitted Sybil. "Some people do seem to have—objectively speaking—a low sexiness quotient. Like my dentist, for example. I mean, he is definitely not sexy."

"Or my aunt," said Ari suddenly.

Sybil nodded. "You're right. I got a good look at her when she was leaving. She's pretty and her clothes and her car are great, but—"

"But something about her makes my flesh creep," said Ari, thinking aloud.

71

Sybil was puzzled. "What do you mean?"

Ari thought of the touch of her aunt's cold lips and her white fingers. She felt herself shudder. "I don't know what I mean." She shook her head. "Forget it."

Kids began pouring out of the refectory. Sybil struggled to her feet. "We'd better get on to class. Here, let me give you my phone number."

Ari watched Sybil write her phone number. The marker she wrote with was black, but still Ari saw the numbers in color—blue, green, yellow. *Maybe I'm losing my mind,* she thought. With a cold feeling in her stomach, she remembered the fanged creatures that had haunted her consciousness only that morning. What made her think she could have a normal life? she wondered. "Give me a call," said Sybil, handing her the folded piece of paper with a smile.

"Sure," said Ari in a hollow voice. "I will."

CHAPTER
SIX

WHEN THE TWINS GOT BACK TO THE HOUSE, THEY learned that Carmel knew only one English phrase—"beauty sleep." She uttered it before disappearing into the kitchen to cook dinner. Aunt Gabrielle, it seemed, was not to be disturbed.

"Okay by me," muttered Paul. "It gives us a chance to poke around the house some by ourselves."

A large Oriental gong gleamed at the end of the hallway. Past the gong was the dining room where they had eaten breakfast. Only now the heavy velvet curtains had been pulled back, and they could see that a garden lay beyond the dining room.

Ari slid open a broad door to her right to reveal an elegant living room with a striped satin sofa and an elaborate white stone fireplace. A gilt clock under a glass dome stood on the mantel. It was decorated in blue and gold with the signs of the zodiac. Paul whistled. "Fancy!"

Ari ran her fingers across the face of the fireplace mantel. "Look at this, Paul."

Paul stooped down to get at eye level with the mantel. "It looks old. Maybe Aunt Gabrielle bought it off some mansion they were tearing down or something."

"Something's carved into it," said Ari.

Paul sat down on the hearth. From that angle, he could see better. A woman's face encircled with acanthus leaves had been carved into the stone. He guessed, judging from the style of simpering prettiness, that it must date from the turn of the century. He had seen Victorian valentines with exactly that sort of cloyingly sweet face. He let his fingers slide across the face. "Wait a minute," he cried. "It moves." Paul nudged the face gently with the heel of his hand. He heard a click and the face pivoted easily in its stone socket to reveal its other side, the carving of a macabre skull, its jaw held on by shreds of rotting flesh. Empty eye sockets stared at Paul. The skull had the wide grin of death, but the most curious thing was that its teeth were bats' teeth, jagged and with two long fangs.

"Horrible!" Ari cried disgustedly. "Why would Aunt Gabrielle want such a thing? Turn it back around so we don't have to look at it."

Paul was in no hurry to turn the skull around. "It must have cost a fortune," he said, frowning at it. "An antique mantel with this sort of shock value would be worth a lot to a collector, wouldn't you think?" He had prowled around New Orleans an-

74

tique shops with his mother and knew about the absurdly high prices of interesting bits of old mansions.

Ari stood up and dusted her hands. "It makes me wonder what other creepy things are hidden around here."

"I wonder where she gets her money," said Paul. "It's not like teaching night classes in college brings in big bucks."

"Well, don't ask her!"

"Like I'm really going to ask her a bunch of personal questions." Paul hesitated. "Well, don't you think we'd better look around some more while we've got the chance?"

Ari shook her head. "I think we ought to go upstairs and lock our doors."

"Oh, come on, Ari. We've got to look around sometime, don't we? I mean, we live here now."

Ari was silent for a moment. "Okay," she said at last.

The twins tiptoed out into the hallway. They heard pans clattering in the kitchen where Carmel was preparing dinner. Ari opened the door across from the living room and peeked in. "Powder room," she said shortly, closing the door. The next room turned out to be a handsome library, its walls lined with books to the ceiling. A ladder on rollers leaned against the shelves.

Ari checked out a few titles. "She's got an awful lot of stuff on Romania and Central Europe, plus a lot that's in French."

"Reference-book-type stuff," Paul concluded.

75

"Books for her teaching." He wasn't sure what led him to the darkest corner of the library. It was as if the brown, untitled book on the shelves there had a magnetic attraction to his fingers. His palms tingled, and for a moment he had the unnerving sensation that his hands were being moved by some unseen force. Jerkily, Paul pulled the book off the shelf.

"What have you got there?" Ari asked.

"I don't know," he said, gazing down at it. The wooden cover was hinged with a brown silk cord, and a woodcut bookplate had been glued on the inside cover. Its darkly inked design showed a globe, a quill pen, and a skull, but something brown had been splotched on it so Paul could not read the name of the book's owner. The pages were heavy, crisp, and smooth, and the writing was in an odd block script. His hands stopped tingling once the book was open. "It's in French," he said, glancing at her. "Can you read it?"

She peered over his shoulder. "It's old French," she said. "See here where it says *teste*? Nowadays they write *tête*."

"How long has it been since they replaced that *s* with the circumflex?"

"I don't know." Ari shrugged "A long time. I think I can make out the gist of it, though. Most of the French isn't all that different."

Paul handed the book to her. He wished he had always done his French homework the way Ari did; all the words they had learned in class swam in his brain. He was never sure whether *quel dommage* meant *too bad* or was a compliment meant for cheese.

Ari scanned the text. "A woman wrote it."

"How can you tell?" asked Paul, peering over her shoulder.

"She calls herself *'blonde,'* with the feminine ending. She's talking about the spring flowers," reported Ari, reading over it swiftly. "She says they smell sweet at night. For some reason she's crazy about night—says it's *plus noir qu'une meure,* blacker than a blackberry." Ari made a face. "Funny way of putting it. She's in love with the moon and she's had good hunting."

"Women don't hunt," protested Paul. "You must be reading it wrong."

"They did in the Middle Ages," retorted Ari. "On those old tapestries of the hunt, there are ladies on horseback with greyhounds and the whole bit." Ari frowned. "Here's another odd line. *'Je vive sans vie.'*" She glanced up at Paul.

"What does it mean?" he asked impatiently.

"I live without life. It doesn't make any sense, does it?" Ari glanced down again at the book and blanched suddenly. "Oh, no! She's hunting peasants, Paul."

"Are you sure you're getting this right?" asked Paul, making a move toward her.

"*Paysan* is peasant. They run from her, but she runs like the wind, she says. She catches them and sinks her teeth into them!"

"Are you sure you're getting this right?" asked Paul.

"*Dents,* that's teeth. She's sucking their blood! It's a vampire's diary, Paul! Put it back on the shelf!" Ari thrust the book at him.

Paul took it from her and held it open gingerly with his thumb.

"Aunt Gabrielle probably has it because she's an expert on Romania," said Ari, grimacing. "Vampires come from Romania. The mountainous part of it used to be called Transylvania. Sybil was telling me that. It's where that girl Nadia comes from."

"But did the nobility in Romania speak French?" asked Paul, puzzled.

"I wish you wouldn't hold your thumb there," said Ari, glancing at him. "That's probably the blood of some poor peasant splashed all over the bookplate."

Paul hastily moved his thumb off of the bookplate and closed the volume. Ari grabbed the book from him and shoved it back into the empty slot in the bookshelf.

"I want to wash my hands," said Ari in a small voice.

Paul froze. His tingling hands felt the wetness of blood, but he looked down at them and they were clean. "Our imaginations are too strong for our own good," he said shakily.

"Why does Aunt Gabrielle have such horrible things in her house?" asked Ari quietly. She shivered. "But it's none of our business. It doesn't have anything to do with us."

Paul wondered if there was any way he could

soak the blood off that bookplate and read the name underneath. Probably not. If it really went as far back as the Middle Ages, the blood might have mixed chemically with the fibers of the parchment. "Maybe we'd better get out of here," he said, glancing uneasily at the brown book.

The other door of the library opened onto the dining room. In the slanting afternoon sunlight, the prisms of the candelabra shot shards of light over the room. Glass-paned doors opened out onto the brick terrace, with its flower beds of roses, azaleas, and sodden petunias. They could hear Carmel humming to herself in the nearby kitchen. A small service hall connected the dining room to the kitchen. Ahead the twins saw a pantry, and just to their right rose a small, dark staircase. "I guess this is the staircase the servants used to use," Ari said.

Paul pushed open the door to a room opposite the narrow staircase.

Carmel stuck her head out of the kitchen. "No, no!" she admonished them, shaking her finger.

Paul quickly closed the door.

"What was in there?" whispered Ari as they left the narrow hallway.

Paul shrugged. "It was just a study. A desk, books, stuff like that. Tall glass doors out to the terrace, kind of like in the dining room."

"What this house needs is a den," Ari said. "With a big color television and some tacky souvenirs from vacations."

Paul grinned. "Yeah, Mickey Mouse dolls from

Disney World and flamingoes made out of seashells."

The twins' footsteps sounded on the marble floor as they ran down the hallway and up the dark staircase to their rooms. Together they fell onto Paul's bed.

Ari sat up. "You know something, Paul? I bet Aunt Gabrielle could get to her study using that back staircase. She could go out the French doors, and we wouldn't even see her leave."

"Why would she want to sneak out of her own house like that?"

"I don't know. It just hit me that this place would be perfect for anybody who had a secret life."

"Your imagination is working overtime again," said Paul.

"We find a skull on the mantel and a vampire's diary in the library and you have the nerve to tell me the trouble is with my imagination?"

"You're right," said Paul, avoiding her eyes. "This place is scary, Ari."

"There's just one other thing I want to check," she said.

She tiptoed out into the hall and Paul trailed after her. Tentatively, she approached the black crow that stood outside Aunt Gabrielle's bedroom. Paul expected her to pick it up; instead, she reached out and touched the obsidian mirror that hung on the wall behind it.

"What—?" Paul exclaimed.

Ari raised her finger to her lips, and he shut up

at once. Neither of them wanted to risk waking Aunt Gabrielle. Ari's hands felt the glassy surface of the black mirror, then groped along the edges of its frame. She gestured to Paul to look, but he couldn't see what she was getting at. The narrow black mirror was built into the woodwork—that was all he could see. Ari took a tissue from her pocket and polished her finger marks off the black surface. The tissue on glass gave a squeak that made them both jump. They tiptoed silently down the blood-red carpet and darted with relief back into Paul's room.

Paul wiped his brow. "What was all that about?" he asked, annoyed at himself for being afraid.

"Most mirrors are hung on the wall with a piece of wire, like a picture," said Ari.

"Some are installed with those little doohickeys," said Paul. "Screws and mirror hangers. So what?"

"Have you *ever* seen one that was built in?"

Paul thought about it. "No. But I'm not sure I've ever seen a black one either. Aunt Gabrielle has weird ideas about interior decoration."

Ari hesitated. "Now promise me you won't laugh at what I'm going to say."

"Ari, I don't think I have a laugh left in me."

"Last night when we came in, I had the sensation I was being watched. What I'm wondering is whether that's a two-way mirror. You know, on one side you get a reflection, but on the other side you see through it like a window."

81

Paul thought about the sinister crow and its reflection in the black glass. He, too, had had the feeling that the crow was looking at him. What if he had been right that something or *someone* was looking at them—someone at the window behind the crow? "Aunt Gabrielle was with us when we came in," he said, puzzled. "Who could have been watching us through that mirror?"

"I don't know," she said. "But I'm sure we were being watched. I felt it, didn't you?"

Paul didn't say anything. He *had* had the same uncomfortable feeling. "But why would anyone want to watch us?"

CHAPTER SEVEN

THE SEMINAR ROOM USED FOR ARI'S AMERICAN LIT class was small and windowless and was completely filled by a round table and chairs. She took the seat next to Cos, who was sprawled over a chair in the corner. He straightened up and pursed his lips appreciatively. One of his legs dangled over the arm of the chair—his black-topped Reebok was within inches of her—and for a second she had trouble catching her breath. The room was so small she had an intoxicating feeling of intimacy, even though she avoided his eyes.

The teacher, Ms. Betancourt, was a slender woman with wispy long hair and bags under her eyes.

It wasn't hard for Ari to follow the class discussion, because she was pretty familiar with Poe's short stories, but she was distracted by Cos's closeness.

It looked as if all her ideas about this new school had been wrong. She had been here only a week but she was already starting to feel at home. With such small classes, it was going to be easier than she thought to get to know people. So far kids hadn't been snobby and standoffish at all— maybe they were glad to see a new face.

After class, Cos cornered her in the hall. "So where are you from?" he murmured, bracing one hand against the wall as he leaned over her. Ari noticed that several Band-Aids were wrapped around his knuckles.

"I'm from New Orleans," said Ari, smiling up at him. "But I'm starting to like it here."

Suddenly a boy came out of the classroom and stared at her for a moment. The blueness of his gaze was startling. Ari averted her eyes uncomfortably, remembering how the boy had introduced himself on her first day in class. *I'm Jessie Driscoll, and I collect guns.*

"Old Jess is the complete paranoid," Cos whispered in Ari's ear. "Don't let it get to you."

"I gotta go, Cos," said Jessie. "If I'm late to Michaels's class again, he's going to dock my grade."

"Go on without me," said Cos. "Come on, Ari. I'll walk you to chemistry."

Ari gave him a startled glance. "How did you know I had chemistry next?"

"Lifted your schedule off the computer," Cos said. "Hey, maybe I shouldn't have told you that. Better for you to think I've got ESP. That touch of mystery, huh?"

"I don't like mysteries," said Ari firmly. "Is Jessie a good friend of yours?" She couldn't help noticing that Jessie had been standing by even while Cos was handing her his line.

"Jessie? Yeah. I guess he is. We go way back. It's not really his fault he's so paranoid. He had a bad experience in South America. His dad is a high-up executive in a banana company that is like some capitalist octopus or something down there. Anyway, Jess was kidnapped by extremists. They thought that was the way to twist his dad's arm, I guess, and have him give away a lot of free bananas. Anyway, the military went house to house, shaking people down and shooting the ones who wouldn't talk, until they found Jess. The extremists didn't actually torture him or anything, but the whole experience made him slightly weird."

"I'm not sure I like people who are weird," said Ari, thinking of her aunt Gabrielle. "Normal is what I go for."

Cos put his arm around her. "Hey, nobody is normal, Ari. Welcome to the real world."

"You seem pretty normal." She gazed up at him.

"I fake it," he said promptly. "Inside I'm weird like everybody else. So, how'd you get to know Sybil?"

"We met at lunch on my first day here. I like her."

"Now, Sybil is weird."

"She's a little blunt, maybe, but I don't think she's weird," said Ari.

Cos laughed. "Nah, I'm kidding. She's great. I like her, too. Well, here's your chemistry class. Have fun." He stopped short of the classroom, pivoted, and abruptly took off running.

When Ari stepped in the classroom, she realized why Cos had lost no time leaving. His girlfriend, Nadia, was by the window. Her black hair was pulled back from her face and fell in a cascade down her back. A few curly wisps clung to her temples. Her teeth were startlingly white. Ari watched her closely, noting her tentative way of moving, her nervous smile. She was so delicate and shy looking, she was like a forest animal. Obviously, Cos wasn't ready to break up with her yet. Otherwise, why had he been so careful to get away before she spotted him?

Paul noticed Sandy MacAdams peering at his sketchbook. "What's that?" Sandy asked.

Paul glanced down at his charcoal drawing. He added fangs to the face in his drawing of a dark man in a cape. The drawing seemed to flow out of his pencil without his thinking about it. It was as if his brain were a transmitter picking up someone else's nightmare.

"Hey, it's a vampire! Not bad!" exclaimed Sandy. "The cape is really good."

The vampire's cape was like Aunt Gabrielle's, Paul thought. The only difference was a stiff collar that stood up behind the vampire's neck.

"Getting in the Halloween spirit, huh?" asked Sandy.

Paul scratched his head. "Guess it shows what kind of mood I'm in, huh?"

He put down his charcoal pencil and gazed at the girl perched on the broad windowsill. Susannah Rodgers. He had seen her name on her portfolio. He loved her little nose and the way she had drawn a line of charcoal makeup slightly upward at the corners of her eyes. Her blond hair was in an untidy knot on top of her head, and the light from the window picked out its silver threads. A gold bangle glimmered on her wrist as her pencil sped over the paper of her sketchbook.

Glancing down at his own drawing, he added a highlight to the vampire's eyes. He shivered. Ever since he had come to Washington, his mind had been flooded with vampires; he wished he could shake the macabre images, but they were vivid and insistent, like a horror film projected on the inside of his skull.

Sandy was peering at everyone else's sketches. He slid up to the window, craned his neck to look at Susannah's sketchpad, then glanced at Paul. He looked from the sketchpad back to Paul several times, then grinned.

Paul blushed. Was Susannah drawing a cartoon of him or something? He wanted to talk to her, but he'd like to make sure first that she wasn't going to blow him off. She was so serene, dreamy even, that it was hard to figure out how to make the first move.

"Take your sketchbooks home, people," said Mrs. Bromley, glancing at her watch. "The more you practice, the better you'll be. Sharpen your eyes. Look at what really is there, not what you think should be there. Expect the unexpected. The artist has a fresh eye."

Expect the unexpected. Mrs. Bromley's words rang in Paul's ears. He felt as if he expected a vampire to jump out at him. He wondered if finding that dead body had done something awful to his nervous system. Sometimes at night when he was falling asleep, he could feel damp blood on his hands. Horrible. He couldn't speak of it, even to Ari.

Chairs scraped against the linoleum floor as kids rose and gathered up their books. Sandy nudged Paul. "You know what Susannah was drawing? She was drawing you, man. You!"

Paul flushed. He would have noticed that Susannah was drawing him if he hadn't been so distracted, he thought.

Paul lingered outside the classroom, hoping Susannah would come out. Then he could at least smile at her and say hi. But she was showing Mrs. Bromley her portfolio. He gazed at a poster outside the classroom door. On it a ghost with cartoon-wide eyes held an orange pumpkin under one arm. "THE BOO BALL," it said. "ANNUAL COSTUME PARTY. COME AS YOUR FAVORITE MONSTER!"

Paul wondered if Susannah had a date for the Boo Ball. He glanced at his watch. He'd better shove off. His ride would be waiting out in front of the school. He hoisted his book bag. It would be good to see Ari, he thought. Without her at his side, he had been feeling oddly incomplete, as if he were listening expectantly for the next note in a song.

But he wasn't looking forward to going back to Aunt Gabrielle's creepy house. He hated the shadowy halls and that stuffed crow with the strangely glittering eyes that seemed to follow him as he walked to his room. *Home, sweet home,* he thought bitterly. No wonder he had been dreaming about vampires.

Ari stepped outside the Lane Building, relieved that the rain had let up. She was sick of trying to figure out the school's confusing maze of corridors. It would be easier to go around on the outside of the classroom buildings, she decided. That way she wouldn't risk getting lost again. The grass was wet and yellow leaves stuck to the cement walk that skirted the building. She shouldered her book bag and set off walking. The overcast skies were ominous. Someone was whistling tunelessly nearby—a gardener maybe? The sound was more like wheezing than like a melody, she thought irritably. She wished he would shut up. She couldn't see whoever it was. The trees and bushes in back were pretty thick. She could make out the shape of the old chapel beyond the thick stand of maples. *Forget going around the entire building,* she thought nervously. She would go in the first door she saw. She hurried, suddenly breathless. It had been a mistake to come outside. Being alone behind the school made her uneasy, almost frightened.

Suddenly there was a harsh cry and the bushes flailed wildly. Ari shied away from them. She backed off the path and onto the grass, then froze, staring at the moving branches. *A cat,* she told herself, trying to still the loud thumping of her heart. Biting her lip, she slowly inched back onto the sidewalk. A brown glimpse of fur caught her eye, and in spite of herself she stooped to look under the tangle of bushes. The dead animal's white teeth showed in a rigid snarl, and its blank eyes stared at her. The cat had been killed. Jumping up suddenly with a gasp, Ari stumbled up the steps of the back entrance to the building and struggled with the doorknob. After what seemed like an eternity, the heavy door swung open, and she slipped inside the building. She was standing near a dark stairwell, but at least she could hear voices. She rushed toward the sounds, past empty class-rooms until she turned the corner and saw people. Talking to some kids, a teacher in a vest leaned against a door. She was safe. But in an uncomfort-able corner of her mind, the cat's death cry echoed. *Some animal has killed it,* she told herself. *A weasel, maybe. Or another cat.*

Ahead of her, Sybil's red-gold hair shone in the gloom of the hallway.

"Sybil!" cried Ari.

Sybil turned around and grinned at her. "Hi! How's it going?"

"I guess I'm pretty tired." Ari ran her fingers through her hair.

"It'll get better when you learn your way

around," Sybil said. "It takes a while." Suddenly she leaned toward her confidentially. "Stephanie Bowers said she saw Cos hit his fist against a brick wall this morning."

"Cos?" exclaimed Ari. Then she remembered the Band-Aids on Cos's fist.

"It happened right outside the library. Nadia took off for class, and then Stephanie saw him turn around and slam his fist into the wall."

"Maybe he's thinking of breaking up with Nadia," Ari said hopefully.

Sybil glanced at her watch. "Maybe. Anyway, I better run. I don't want the car pool to leave me. Give me a call, okay?" She dashed off.

Ari stared at a nearby poster on the wall. "COME TO THE BOO BALL! A COSTUME EXTRAVAGANZA. THRILLS. CHILLS. EXCITEMENT." On the sign, a jack-o'-lantern sneered at a black cat.

Ari shivered and hurried away down the corridor. She opened a door to the outside, but it led only to trees and a playing field. Kids dressed for track were converging there, and for a moment she thought she heard the whistling again. She hurried away down a confusing tangle of hallways and tried another door. To her relief, from this door she could see the circular drive that ran in front of the Schuler Building. Paul was there, standing by the car. Ari ran to him. The Mercedes's engine idled quietly at the curb, but Aunt Gabrielle wasn't inside. It was Carmel who was behind the wheel.

"Are you okay?" asked Paul. He looked into

Ari's eyes and saw the fear there. "What's wrong?" he demanded.

Ari had decided not to tell Paul about the dead cat. She already felt stupid that she had gotten so upset about it.

"I don't know my way around yet—I keep getting lost." She let her voice trail off.

They got in the car and slammed the car doors shut. Ari could feel herself relaxing. Now that she and Paul were together, her spinning wheels had wound down. "How did your day go?" she asked.

"Not bad," Paul said.

Ari leaned forward. "Is Aunt Gabrielle still sleeping?" she asked Carmel in a loud, slow voice.

"*Que?*" replied Carmel.

"Never mind." Ari sighed and fell back against the leather cushions. She did know a few words in Spanish—*feliz navidad, tortilla*. But they wouldn't get her far in an actual conversation.

Autumn leaves made a vivid splash of color against the gray sky. Around the circular drive, kids from St. Anselm's were piling into station wagons piloted by mothers in sweaters and tweed jackets.

The Mercedes pulled out onto busy Massachusetts Avenue. A Metro Bus pulled noisily ahead of them, spouting diesel fumes.

Paul said abruptly, "Do you have Susannah Rogers in any of your classes?"

"Blond hair, perfect nails? I know the one you mean. She's in my chemistry class. The complete bimbo."

92

Paul flushed. "Jeez, Ari, do you have to be so critical of every girl I even mention?"

"I'm not critical," said Ari promptly. "I'm observant. But don't stop—go on. I'm interested. Exactly what is it you like about her?"

"I'm not sure," Paul said. "But she's definitely got something."

"She's got perfect nails," said Ari.

"I'm not exactly crazy about what's-his-face, either," Paul pointed out.

Ari opened her mouth to protest, but suddenly the silliness of their sniping at each other struck her. She looked at Paul and they both laughed.

"Truce?" said Paul.

"Okay," agreed Ari. "I won't say anything about the bimbo if you won't say anything about Cos."

The bimbo crack was not in keeping with the spirit of a truce, but Paul decided to let it go by.

"Cos walked me to chemistry today," Ari said. Outside, behind a black iron fence, she saw thick trees and gently rolling green lawns. A white cement anchor marked the U.S. Naval Observatory.

"Honestly, that guy is so full of himself," muttered Paul. "He only just met you and already he's closing in for the kill."

"Self-confidence is a good thing," said Ari.

Paul knew he was being petty. He needed to get a life. He gazed out the window. A girl on a bicycle passed them. The traffic moved slowly. "You know, this guy, Sandy, told me that they hardly take any transfers into the fifth form." Paul glanced at his twin. "He wanted to know whether

93

I was some kind of genius or whether my family had pull."

"I guess you told him you were a genius, right?" said Ari.

"Very funny," said Paul.

"The trouble is," said Ari with a frown, "we don't know anything about what kind of pull Aunt Gabrielle has. We don't know anything at all about her. Nothing."

"It was pretty clear she was chummy with the headmaster," Paul pointed out. "And she did say our dad used to go to St. Anselm's."

"I guess that could be it," said Ari, shivering a little. "Some kind of old boy network."

The Mercedes passed the grand iron gates of the British Embassy where the statue of Churchill stood. "You know, I think this new town is going to work out for us," said Paul, smiling. "All these embassies and flags—it makes you feel like anything could happen, doesn't it? Like the city's probably full of spies and all." He glanced at his twin. "It's kind of exciting."

Ari had felt that way herself earlier in the day. But since she had encountered the dead cat, her mood had changed. "I've had about all the excitement I can take for a while," she said.

But Paul felt his spirits rising. He figured Aunt Gabrielle would let him borrow the car for the dance. Or better yet, maybe she would get him a car of his own. "Well, I think this is really a neat city," he said.

The streets were beginning to take on a recognizable Georgetown look. Brick sidewalks. Restaurants. Antique stores. Ari gazed doubtfully at the expensive shops. "I guess it's okay for people who've got money and influence," she said.

Paul laughed. "We've got both now, don't we?"

CHAPTER
EIGHT

THE NEXT MORNING WHEN PAUL'S ROOM WAS GRAY with the first morning light, he looked down at the foot of his bed and saw that a lady in a long green velvet dress was sitting at his desk, writing with a quill pen. Her eyes looked feverishly hot, and her forehead was unnaturally high, as if she had plucked out the first inch or so of her hair. Her odd headdress, a soft white cloth draped over a tall twin-peaked frame, moved softly as she wrote. Her skin was the same dead-white color as her head-dress. Long blond hair streamed thinly to her waist.

The wardrobe opened and a muscular man stepped out, lifting his blue cape to keep the velvet from catching on the wood. The man wore a plate-sized fur hat, and Paul could see that either he had shaved his head or he was bald—the bulging bones of his skull showed under his shiny white skin. His cape's material puckered where it had been heavily embroidered with gold asterisks. A large hound leapt out of the wardrobe after him. The hound's heavy jowls and ears swung slightly as it lurched toward Paul's bed. Its flesh hung loosely on its bones, and he could see that its eyes were ruby-colored and bloodshot. It snuffled at him, and he could feel its breath on his toes.

The caped man pulled open Paul's dresser drawer and tossed Paul's underwear to the floor. The man and woman looked at him, as if daring him to protest, and grinned suddenly. He saw then that they had fangs. The woman's white, glistening fangs pressed against her thin lower lip, denting the flesh. Paul opened his mouth to scream, but no sound came out. He heard Ari's alarm go off, and as if they had been frightened by the sound, the figures grew thin and vanished.

Paul sat up in bed abruptly, his heart pounding in fear. It was a minute or two before he could force himself to get out of bed. When he did, the cold floor felt reassuringly real under his bare feet. He padded over to the dresser, bent down to pick up a pair of underwear, and tossed it back in the drawer. He must have dropped it last night without noticing, he told himself.

Paul wasn't sure what made him go over to his desk. The vampire's quill pen had disappeared, but something had been written on the paper blotter in odd block letters. *"Je m'appelle Blanche."*

He could feel a cold sweat breaking on his forehead. "My name is Blanche." He had enough

French to decipher the words, but the problem was those words shouldn't even have been there—the vampire lady had existed only in his imagination!

That line could have been there for months or even years, he told himself wildly. Some maid had been practicing her French lesson. Or a guest of Aunt Gabrielle's could have written it. There could be a hundred logical explanations. He tore the top sheet of paper off the blotter, crumpled it, and tossed it into the trash.

Days passed before Paul could think of his strange vision without shaking. He was tempted to tell Ari about it, but he couldn't bring himself to. He was weighed down by the memory of it and by the sensation of blood on his hands, which made it difficult for him to focus and concentrate at school. He kept seeing Ari in the hall with Cos, laughing, flirting, looking happy. He hated the idea that Ari might be mentally comparing him to Cos, who seemed to walk around in his own private beam of sunshine. Worse yet, Paul thought, if he told Ari about his visions, she might even confide in Cos about her troubled brother. The thought made him shudder.

Paul worked hard on his French lessons without quite acknowledging to himself that he'd like to have another go at deciphering the strange diary in Aunt Gabrielle's library. Things could have been worse, he told himself. He was getting to know some people at school—Sandy, Susannah.

He was pretty sure that Susannah liked him. He was finding his way around okay.

The following week when Paul's English class went to the library to do research, he found a dark corner and combed the card catalogue for everything it had to offer on visions and hallucinations. He came up with a stack of books and periodicals and began plowing through them. As he read, his mind cleared.

He regretted that he had pitched the crumpled paper in the trash. Carmel had presumably carried it out to the curb in the normal course of things, and it was buried in a landfill somewhere. He was feeling calmer now about his strange vision. But nagging at the back of his mind was the thought that he could have compared the writing with the writing in the vampire diary in Aunt Gabrielle's library.

The phone beside Paul's bed rang suddenly before dinner one night and he grabbed it.

"It's probably for me," said Ari. "Sybil wanted me to call her."

"Hullo?" said Paul. "Yeah, just a minute." He handed Ari the receiver. "It's not Sybil," he said flatly.

"I'll take it in my room," Ari said. She stepped into her bedroom and picked up the phone.

"Ari? It's Cos."

Ari waited until she heard Paul hang up before she spoke. "Just a minute, Cos. Let me close the door."

She used to let me listen to everything she said to boys, Paul thought, watching the connecting door swing closed. He heard the click as it snapped shut. It sounded in his heart like a bell of loneliness. He discovered that he hated Cos.

Ari snuggled her bare feet under the bed-spread. The prisms on her bedside lamp twinkled gaily.

"How did you get my number?" she asked Cos.

"It's on the computer," he said. "Piece of cake."

"Good grief! What else about me is on the computer?"

"I know your dearest, darkest secrets," Cos intoned. "I know your deepest secret fears."

Ari gulped, thinking suddenly of the fanged creatures of her dreams and the odd whiteness of Aunt Gabrielle's taut skin. "All of that is on the computer?" she said faintly.

"Nah. I'm just kidding. Have you read 'The Tell-Tale Heart' yet?"

"Not yet," said Ari, eyeing her book bag uneasily. Somehow, now that she was living in Aunt Gabrielle's dark house, the last thing in the world she wanted to do was to read a scary Poe story. She was afraid she would jump clear out of her skin. "What about you?" she asked. "Have you read it?"

"Yup, but don't tell anybody. I make out like I never study, because then when I get an *A* people think I'm smart. But why are we talking about schoolwork? Do you know what you were wearing the first time I saw you?" Cos asked. He recited every detail of Ari's outfit from her ribbed navy tights to the black pearl buttons on her shirt.

"What a memory you've got!" She laughed.

"I'm obsessed."

Ari didn't reply. The line was silent for a few seconds.

"What's wrong?" Cos asked at last.

"I'm thinking about Nadia," said Ari. "Aren't you supposed to be going with her?"

Another long silence fell on the telephone line.

"I've got to let Nadia down easy," Cos said at last.

Ari's heart squeezed in disappointment. Cos should have broken up with Nadia by now. He had been walking with Ari to class for weeks, but she noticed that he always took care not to run into Nadia. He must have been more deeply entangled than she had guessed.

"You know what?" asked Cos, abruptly changing the subject. "My dad is already riding me about colleges. Is that grim or what? Sometimes I feel like throwing myself under a bus. Do you ever get depressed, Ari? I mean black, black depressed."

"Yes," Ari said softly. "My mother was killed in a car wreck. That's why we came here to live with our aunt."

"I'm sorry," said Cos after a few seconds. "I didn't know."

"Yes," said Ari in a small voice. "I wish she was alive so much I can't stand it. It's so awful it seems like it can't have happened to us. But it did."

"What about your dad? Where's he?"

"He's out of the picture," said Ari. "Paul and I don't even remember what he looks like."

"That's tough," said Cos.

"Well, Paul and I have got each other," said Ari, a lump growing in her throat. "And Aunt Gabrielle, of course," she added as an afterthought.

"I wish I could put my arms around you and kiss those tears away," said Cos.

Ari smiled sadly to herself. Cos didn't understand that some tears are too deep to kiss away.

"You still there?" asked Cos anxiously.

"Still here," she said.

"Jeez, that's my mom's calling me. Look, I better go. See you tomorrow."

Ari sat on her bed a minute, thinking. If she wanted Cos, it was going to take careful handling. She didn't want to scare him off by pushing him to break up with Nadia, but on the other hand, she had to make it clear at some point that Nadia was going to have to go. This was the modern world—boys didn't have harems.

Ari got up and knocked on the connecting door. Paul opened the door. "So, how's what's-his-face?" he asked sourly.

"I think he's in deep with that girlfriend of his," said Ari. "I don't know what's going to happen."

"Is he?" asked Paul, looking more cheerful. "Gee, that's too bad."

The gong sounded downstairs.

The twins filed down the sweeping staircase and

went into the dining room. Carmel brought steaming casseroles to the dining room table. Her face was pink from the heat of the kitchen. The twins sat down, uncertain whether to begin eating or not. Then Aunt Gabrielle appeared at the door. She was wearing a luminescent pink jacket, shiny tights, and a baseball cap that cast a mask of shadow over her eyes so that her strange half-smile looked even more enigmatic. "I've already had a bite to eat," she said. "You two go ahead. I'm off on my evening jog."

"Are you sure it's a good idea for you to keep jogging by yourself after dark?" Paul asked.

"I'm perfectly safe!" Aunt Gabrielle ran a few steps in place. "I have my pepper spray." She whipped a small metal canister out of her jacket pocket. "And I'm an a aikido master," she added. "So don't worry." She gave a low throaty chuckle. "Of course, if I catch either of you going out alone after dark you'll be grounded for the rest of your life. Ta, kids!" She jogged down the long hallway and disappeared out the front door.

"It's always the same," said Paul. "Have you noticed that? It's do as I say, not as I do. Remember how Mom used to sneak smokes in the backyard? And then she told us she'd kill us if she ever caught us with a cigarette."

"That was for our own good," said Ari. She wiped her eyes with the corner of a napkin.

"Ari, don't start," said Paul. "You'll have us both bawling."

Ari blew her nose. "I'm fine. Perfectly fine. Pass me the salad."

Paul passed her the salad, then dipped himself a serving of paella. "Did you hear Aunt Gabrielle say she had 'a bite to eat'? She probably ate a carrot. It's no wonder she's so skinny. I'm not sure I've ever actually seen her eat anything."

Ari thought about how diet checklists, scales, and pamphlets entitled "How to Lose Ten Pounds in Two Weeks" had littered their kitchen at home. Their mother had been trying to lose twenty pounds for what seemed like forever. But her lap was perfect for sitting on, and her bosom was perfect for snuggling. Ari couldn't imagine snuggling up against Aunt Gabrielle.

When Aunt Gabrielle got back, Paul was forced to admit that the exercise had done her good. Her corpse-pale skin always had a warm glow when she came back. But he still thought it was funny the way she went jogging at night. It was a part of her inflexible routine, like the way she slept nearly every day until sunset and stuck to it even on beautiful days. He kept having the feeling that something strange was behind it, the way the strange hidden skull was behind the simperingly pretty face on the mantel.

"You look great," said Ari. "Maybe I should take up jogging myself."

Aunt Gabrielle pinched Ari's cheek playfully, and Ari winced at her touch. "You don't need to jog, sweetest," she said. "You're perfect the way you are." She stripped off her cap and inhaled deeply.

"Aunt Gabrielle," said Ari, "we're going to have a party at school for Halloween. Do you think Paul and I could get some costumes?"

Aunt Gabrielle brightened. "What fun! I know the perfect little man—a real artist. He has a delightful shop down by the canal. You must go by and see him." She cocked her head at them. "Another thing. I almost forgot. Paul, Carmel's not going to come in early tomorrow, so if you'd like, you and Ari can drive the Mercedes to school. Do you think you can find your way?"

"Sure!" Paul said.

"This weekend, we'll have to get a car for you children to use. But I won't need mine tomorrow except to drive to my classes in the evening, so you might as well use it."

Imagining himself driving up to school in the black Mercedes, Paul felt his spirits lifting. Good food, the chance to drive a great car, and on top of that a pretty girl at school who seemed to like him—he could be in worse shape. But suddenly his gaze met Aunt Gabrielle's, and he was struck by the oddness of her lavender eyes. Was it only the way the light hit them, or had they actually begun to glow? Paul shivered and hastily looked away.

CHAPTER
NINE

THE FOLLOWING MORNING, HOWEVER, AS PAUL PULLED up to the gatehouse at the main entrance to the school, he was not quite so sure his luck was improving. It turned out that only seniors could park on campus. It took him a long time to find a parking place, and it was blocks away from the school. The twins hoisted their heavy book bags and trudged uphill to St. Anselm's. "I'm beginning to see why practically everyone belongs to car pools," said Paul.

"I can't imagine Aunt Gabrielle driving a car pool," said Ari.

"Then I guess we look for a parking place every morning and walk a mile uphill," said Paul.

Ahead of them stood the chapel and the thick trees that clustered in front of it. "Let's don't go across the back of the school," Ari said suddenly. "Let's go around the front way."

"Are you nuts?" Paul stared at her. "It's twice as far to go around that way."

Ari didn't argue with him. She set her jaw and struck off along the drive. Paul swore a second or two, then ran and caught up with her. "What's going on with you?" he asked.

"I saw a dead cat back there once," she said.

Paul laughed. "Good grief, Ari. Cats die all the time. Everything dies sooner or later. A dead cat's no big deal."

"Shut up!" she cried. "Stop it!"

"I'm sorry," Paul said, watching her face. "We'll go the long way around. No problem."

Someone had piled stacks of hay and pumpkins in front of the Schuler Building. A sign advertising the Boo Ball was propped up on the hay, wedged between two pumpkins.

"Let's coordinate our costumes for the Boo Ball, Paul," said Ari suddenly. "Remember when we were six, and we were Raggedy Ann and Andy?"

"Actually," Paul said. "I was thinking about asking Susannah to go with me."

"Oh. No problem," Ari said, looking let down. "I can probably go with Sibyl."

Later that morning, Ari was mounting the dark staircase in the Lane Building when she met Nadia coming down. Nadia backed against the wall and crossed herself, muttering something under her breath.

"Hello?" Ari said.

But Nadia only opened her mouth wide, like a

gaping goldfish, then closed it. Her teeth and the whites of her eyes were startlingly bright in the gloom of the staircase. She turned around suddenly and ran back up the stairs.

"Well," muttered Ari. "Good morning to you, too."

Ari felt strange, as if Nadia had somehow picked up on something that was wrong with her. She knew Nadia's snub was getting to her only because her nerves were rubbed raw, but she couldn't help herself. She stepped into the girls' room and checked herself in the mirror. A thin light filtered in the high frosted windows of the room, giving her a ghostly look. What was she expecting? she wondered. To find out that she had sprouted fangs?

At lunch Ari told Sybil about her strange encounter with Nadia on the dark staircase.

"She actually crossed herself?" asked Sybil incredulously. "Jeez, do you think she knows about you and Cos?"

Ari poured herself some apple juice. "How can she? Nothing much has happened between me and Cos. Not yet, anyway."

"Maybe she foresees that he's going to dump her for you," said Sybil. "Somebody told me she's got second sight. She's from Romania, you know."

"So you told me," said Ari irritably. "Romania's all I seem to hear about lately."

Sybil gave a sinister chuckle. "Dracula! Vampires! Maybe Nadia's related to Count Dracula or something." She grabbed a roll from the bread basket. "I think her family used to have a castle in the mountains over there or something."

Ari didn't respond. Sybil's remarks about vampires had given her an uneasy feeling in her stomach.

"Very Halloweenish, isn't it?" said Sybil. "Hey, you want to go to the Boo Ball?"

"I'd love to," said Ari, taking a deep breath. "This isn't one of those things where everybody's got a date, is it?"

"Oh, it won't be like that at all," Sybil assured her. "Half the fun is not knowing who anybody is. I mean, everybody's kissing everybody else and making out in the bushes. But since we're all in masks, it's all very confusing, and nobody gets committed to anything. It's great! And the costumes are *spectacular*. You've got to be careful what you decide to be, though. Last year somebody went as a pack of cards and they couldn't sit down all night."

"So everybody wears masks?" asked Ari.

"Yep. Of course, people still sort of guess who's who," admitted Sybil. "But really, the costumes are incredible. People go all out. I don't know where people get some of these things. Last year, Jessie came in a full suit of armor!"

"How did you know it was him?" asked Ari.

Sybil blushed. "Well, at one point, he, uh, did lift up his visor."

Ari wouldn't kiss Jessie if he were the last boy on earth. She'd always be wondering if he had a gun stashed on him somewhere.

"If Cos is going to dump Nadia," Ari said

109

under her breath, "I wish he'd go ahead and do it."

"Boys!" sighed Sybil.

That night at dinner, the candelabra on the buffet burned with steady electric light. Ari thought it was odd that Aunt Gabrielle used fake candles wired for little electric bulbs. It seemed so tacky, and everything else about the house looked expensive and elegant.

"Our family has always been liberal," said Aunt Gabrielle, pushing a tidbit of food around on her china plate. "I hate to say it, but some people of our sort," she made a face, "are almost fascist. Even positively predatory. When it comes right down to it, they want to decide things *for* other people. Our family has never believed in that."

Ari was a little unclear what Aunt Gabrielle was talking about. How could anyone decide something for someone else? It wasn't as if the U.S. was a dictatorship.

"What about our father?" said Paul. "Is he a liberal, too?"

Aunt Gabrielle winced. "Well, dear, Richard is so unconventional, it's hard to fit him into any pattern."

A drunk, Paul translated mentally. He had begun to suspect that his father might have a drinking problem. Aunt Gabrielle's evasiveness whenever his father's name came up seemed to confirm his suspicions.

"Aunt Gabrielle, I've been thinking I'd like to get my teeth capped," Ari said, eager to avoid the subject of their father.

"Your teeth?" Aunt Gabrielle looked surprised.

Ari bared her teeth. "The canines," she said. "Most people, in case you haven't noticed, have smooth ones. Mine are pointy."

Aunt Gabrielle folded her napkin. "Oh, really, Ari. I can't approve of filing down perfectly good teeth. At least not while you're so young. Who knows but in a few years you might regret it? Anyone for dessert? Carmel has fixed some lovely flan."

"I could eat dessert," said Paul.

Aunt Gabrielle smiled at him. Ari wondered if Aunt Gabrielle herself had pointed incisors and that was why she had that funny Mona Lisa smile that showed no teeth. Aunt Gabrielle got up to go into the kitchen to tell Carmel they were ready for dessert. As she pushed the door open, Spanish floated out of the kitchen.

"I bet she's had six kinds of plastic surgery," said Ari heatedly. "Face lifting, tummy tucking, liposuction, the works. I don't see what's the big deal about getting my teeth capped."

"What's wrong with your teeth?" asked Paul. "They're just like mine."

Ari cast a nervous glance toward the kitchen. "Paul, do you ever have . . . funny dreams?"

"Sometimes," he admitted cautiously.

Aunt Gabrielle returned smiling. "What a lovely, lovely flan Carmel has made for you two!" she said. "It's such a joy to see healthy young appetites."

"Aren't you going to have any, Aunt Gabrielle?"

Paul shot a glance at Ari. The way Aunt Gabrielle picked at her food was a joke between them.

"None for me tonight," said Aunt Gabrielle. "I'm saving my calories for tomorrow. The caterers and the florist's men will probably be here by the time you get in from school." She waved her thin hand, and her diamond rings glittered. "I'm having a little soiree."

Catered dinner parties with fresh flowers did not come cheap, Ari knew. "Aunt Gabrielle," she asked suddenly, "where does our family's money come from?"

Aunt Gabrielle looked at her blankly.

"You know," Ari continued stubbornly, "like at school Jessie's dad is a bigwig in the banana industry, and Nadia's family has a castle in Transylvania somewhere. I just wondered where our family's money comes from."

"Wise investments, my dear," said Aunt Gabrielle firmly. She glanced toward the kitchen. "Oh, look! Here comes Carmel with that lovely flan!"

CHAPTER
TEN

AFTER DINNER, ARI TOOK OFF FOR SYBIL'S. PAUL WAS
sure she and Sybil planned to hash out the entire
business with Cos word by word. It used to be that
Ari talked to *him* about the boys who had crushes
on her. But Cos was different. That was becoming
pretty obvious.

But if she can have her secrets, so can I,
thought Paul with satisfaction. He had his own
plan for tonight, and it was something he had no
intention of sharing with Ari. When Aunt
Gabrielle went upstairs to put on her jogging
clothes, Paul went upstairs directly after her and
changed into black jeans, a turtleneck, and a black
leather jacket. He peeked out his bedroom door
and saw Aunt Gabrielle, all in pink, headed for the
stairs. He waited until she had had time to get outside; then he pulled a dark knit cap low over his
ears and took off after her. He reached the front

door breathless with anxiety. But when he stepped outside, she was still in sight, hesitating at the corner traffic light.

He galloped down the steps and took off after her. He was careful to jog close to the buildings so he could take cover in a doorway or an alley if she looked back. But she didn't look back. His sneakers thudded softly on the brick sidewalks as he jogged at a safe distance behind her. He noticed that passersby avoided his path. His black clothes and dark knit cap made him look like a mugger.

The sidewalk grew crowded. People were getting out of their cars and going into restaurants. He passed a bunch of college students starting the weekend early, singing as they staggered along the sidewalk. Still it was easy to keep Aunt Gabrielle in sight. Her fluorescent jogging gear was like a pink beacon ahead of him.

Paul began to lose track of where he was as she zigzagged through the streets, but he had the vague sense they were heading down toward the desolate canal and harbor area. He was not enthusiastic about jogging in that neighborhood at night. It was deserted, Paul thought uneasily. But he was not about to give up at this point. He kept after her doggedly, then all of a sudden he lost her. He stopped dead in his tracks for an instant in sheer surprise. She had seemed to disappear into thin air. He took off running and skidded to a stop at the lamppost where he had lost sight of her.

Patrons were spilling out of a neon-lit bar onto the sidewalk in front of Paul. Just beyond the bar was a narrow alley. Paul peered down it, noting the glitter of broken glass on the ground. *She couldn't have gone down the alley,* he decided. There was barely space to squeeze through, much less to run. He glanced dubiously into the teeming bar. Perhaps she had nipped into the bar for a drink, he thought. He could have used a glass of water himself, and he had done long-distance running for years and was presumably in a lot better shape than Aunt Gabrielle was. He hesitated for a moment. He was five years underage, but the bar did not look to him like the sort of place that would check I.D.'s. He squeezed through the crowd at the door and found himself suddenly engulfed in a bear hug.

"Rich!" cried a deep voice. "Where've you been?" Paul struggled free of the man's grasp and stared at the bearded face of a huge fellow draped in gold chains. "Excuse me!" the man said, startled. "I thought you were a friend of mine."

Paul felt trapped by the press of the crowd in the dark bar. Most of them were wearing thin, shiny clothes, and he kept getting pressed uncomfortably against bracelets and chains. Feeling hot and conspicuous, he tore off his knit cap. At once a woman sitting on a bar stool ruffled his hair.

"Where've you been, lover?" she asked. She had a foreign accent, maybe Dutch. Surprised, Paul wheeled around to face her and was embarrassed to see that her thin white blouse, unbuttoned to the waist, hardly covered her at all. He could see the ribs in her bony chest under the thin material.

She was very thin and pale, with straight blond hair that fell in bangs to her nose and splayed carelessly over her shoulders. "Why, you're a kid!" she said, laughing. She covered her mouth suddenly with a bony, jewel-encrusted hand. She reached out and touched his forehead with one finger, laughed again, and Paul saw a flash of fangs. He blinked and they were gone.

An optical illusion, he told himself, badly shaken.

He looked around, but did not see Aunt Gabrielle. It had been stupid to come in here, he thought. This wasn't her sort of place. He pushed his way to the less crowded back of the bar. There a rotating light made him dizzy. Suddenly he was jerked off his feet by powerful hands. "Caught up with you at last, Richard," a man growled. A sudden blow from nowhere sent a blinding pain through Paul's jaw. The rotating light doubled suddenly. Paul shook his head to clear it, and his knees buckled with the pain. He was dimly aware of the feel of a door against his back and of screams of protest.

"That's not Richard," cried a high voice in a Dutch accent. "You're beating up on some kid!"

Paul felt a doorknob under his fingers, twisted it, and fell outside into the darkness of a back alley. He lay propped on his elbows a moment, feeling sick. A shaft of light came out through the cracked door, and he could see that he was sitting on a handful of discarded newspaper. A rotting cabbage lay nearby. At least, he thought, he was

116

not still seeing double. Whoever hit him hadn't come after him. His head felt terrible and he wasn't sure he should stand up.

He rolled over and found himself nose to nose with a news story. "BODY FISHED OUT OF CANAL." The paper recounted that the murder victim had bled to death when his carotid artery had been severed by a jagged instrument. "The serial killer!" Paul said aloud, astonished.

He thought about taking the newspaper back to show Ari, but it was wet and smelled of cabbages. It was going to be hard enough, he thought, fingering his jaw, to get himself home.

As he limped back to N Street, moving slowly and carefully, Paul wondered if Aunt Gabrielle had somehow spotted him and had deliberately tried to lose him. That would explain her zigzag path through the streets. Was he wrong to think that it was odd for a woman to jog through dark city streets every night? Still, no matter how he tried to talk himself out of it, there *was* something peculiar about Aunt Gabrielle's appetite for nighttime jogging.

When Paul got back to the house, instead of going in the front door, he opened the garden gate and slipped around the back way. He went in the back door through the dining room, then after a moment's hesitation, began mounting the servants' dark staircase. Aunt Gabrielle might have made it back to the house before him, and he didn't want her to realize that he had been tailing her. He wanted to get out of his black clothes before she saw him.

The dark and narrow staircase made him nervous, but at least no stairs creaked under his feet. The trouble was, he wasn't sure where it ended up on the second floor. Remembering Ari's theory about their aunt's secret life, he was worried that it would end smack in Aunt Gabrielle's bedroom.

When he reached the second landing, he was confronted with two doors at right angles to each other. He stood there for a moment, wondering which one he should try. The landing was dark, and he could see only faint cracks of light under the doors. He heard the muffled sound of running water and a swishing sound, and he smiled. Aunt Gabrielle must be washing out her delicate things in her bathroom. He had heard those sounds often enough back in New Orleans when Ari was tying up the only bathroom in the house washing cotton sweaters. Relieved, he chose the other door and found that it opened onto the hallway. He was only a few steps from his own bedroom. Breathlessly, he slipped into his room and began stripping off his clothes.

"Paul?" Ari's voice sounded frightened.

He pulled on his blue jeans and peeked in her room. "Hi." He smiled, trying to clear his head. "What's up?"

"Where have you been?" she cried. "When I got back from Sybil's you weren't anywhere around. I was worried sick."

"You didn't tell Aunt Gabrielle, did you?" he asked quickly.

"Of course not," she said. "But where were you,

Paul? You look awful! Your hair is all messed up!"

Paul ran his fingers through it and watched a bit of cabbage leaf fall to the floor.

Ari touched his face and he winced. "What happened to you?" she asked incredulously.

"You think I'm going to get a bruise?" he asked. "Somebody hit me. I was trailing Aunt Gabrielle, but I lost her. I went into this bar, thinking she had gone in there, and the next thing I knew some guy was belting me." He gave a wry smile, then thought better of it. His head was still ringing with pain. "He mistook me for some guy named Richard."

Paul had intended to tell Ari then about the news item that reminded him of the serial killer, but what she said next knocked that thought clear out of his mind.

"You must have been right about us looking like our dad, Paul," said Ari, wide-eyed. "I'll bet that's who he got you mixed up with."

Paul blinked. He was used to hearing his father's name pronounced in the French way, "Ree-shar." That was the way Aunt Gabrielle said it. He felt so stupid. He hadn't even made the connection. The woman at the bar had seemed to be on intimate terms with this "Richard," yet she had mixed the two of them up. And so had the guy who hugged him at the door. "Rich," he had called him. "I thought you were a friend of mine," he had said. Then there was the guy who belted Paul.

"Maybe I found out something tonight after all," he said slowly.

CHAPTER
ELEVEN

WHEN ARI'S GAZE DARTED FEARFULLY AROUND THE dimly lit room the next morning, she saw no sign of the fanged creatures. She sighed in relief. But then the curtains stirred, and from behind them stepped a tabby-striped cat that seemed to grow larger as it approached, fluffing its fur. It hissed at her and drew up its snout to show two pointed teeth and a rough pink tongue. Its glowing green eyes rolled back in fear. Suddenly its back arched. It let out a human scream and leapt up onto Ari's knees. Its hair stood on end as if it had been electrified. Ari felt its claws and squirmed frantically to get away. With a thump she fell out of bed, entangled in her sheets.

The door flew open and Paul ran in. "Ari?" he cried. "Are you all right?"

Ari scrambled up. Her heart pounding, she patted the sheets and bedspread. The cat had vanished.

"I guess I had a nightmare," she said. "It was horrible." She got down on her knees and peered under her bed, holding her breath and half-expecting to see green cat's eyes glowing at her from the darkness. "I don't know what I'm looking for," she said.

"I heard this awful sound—" Paul began.

"You heard something?" asked Ari, looking up at him quickly.

"I heard a loud thump. It must have been you falling out of bed."

Ari stood up. She didn't know whether she was relieved or not that Paul hadn't heard the cat's strangely human scream.

"Hey," said Paul. "Come here." He held out his arms.

Ari leaned her head against his shoulder and let him stroke her hair. "You know how you can take an aspirin for a headache?" she whimpered. "I wish there were something you could take for . . . nightmares."

"Yeah. Me, too," he said softly.

When she looked up at him, she could see that a bruise was swelling on his jaw, making the skin there puffy and shiny.

"Does it hurt?" she asked.

"What? Oh, this." He touched his jaw gingerly. "Yeah. Especially when I think about it. That guy was pretty mad at Richard, whoever he was. Wouldn't you figure that meant he'd seen him pretty recently?"

Ari thought about it. "I don't know. Sometimes people hold grudges for a long time."

"Well, I think it means our dad is in town," said Paul.

"Why hasn't he come by to see us, then?" asked Ari.

Paul didn't respond.

"It doesn't matter to us whether he's here or in Timbuktu if he doesn't care about seeing us," Ari said quickly. "You know it's the truth, Paul."

Paul turned away. "I'd just like to see him and . . . tell him what I think of him," he said thickly.

In one of those flashes in which the twins read each other's mind, Ari heard in Paul the anger booming, and over it the thin violin strain of longing and hope. She wished she could tell their father what she thought of him, too. She herself had given up on him long ago, but she hated him for what he was doing to Paul.

Cos was waiting for Ari when she got to school. He put both hands on her shoulders and backed her up against a wall. "I broke up with Nadia," he said. "Will you go to the Boo Ball with me?"

"I'm going with Sybil," said Ari.

"She can come with us," said Cos unhesitatingly.

"I didn't think the Boo Ball was one of those things where people take dates," Ari said.

He looked stricken. "Are you telling me you don't want to go with me?"

"Sure, I'll go with you," she said. "But we have to take Sybil."

"I like Sybil. So that's fine. Besides, it's not the

kind of thing where everybody pairs off."

She hesitated and glanced up at him. "So why are you asking me, then?"

His eyes looked haunted. "I think I need to sort of solidify this breakup with Nadia," he said. "Like, you and me have to go somewhere public together so she gets the message that we really are finished."

"But we'll be in disguise. She won't even know we're together."

"Everybody will guess who we are." He put his hand under her chin, leaned close, and kissed her on the lips.

"More solidifying of the breakup with Nadia?" she asked sweetly.

"Is that a nice thing to say when a guy kisses you?" he asked.

Ari smiled warmly at him, and reassured, he drew her close to him until his breath tickled her ear. Then he pressed his lips against hers again in a long kiss that made her breath come fast. Her toes were warm and that morning's nightmare suddenly seemed far away. But Ari forced herself to pull away from him just the same. Cos had only recently broken up with Nadia. It didn't seem tactful for them to make out in public so soon. "What are you going as?" she asked.

"What?"

"The Boo Ball? What are you wearing?"

"I'm not telling." He grinned. "It ought to be a surprise."

"How will I know it's you? I could end up

going to the party with the wrong guy."

"Come on! Do you really think you could get me mixed up with somebody else?"

She shook her head, smiling. She knew she couldn't get him mixed up with anyone else in the world.

Ari couldn't wait to tell Sybil that Cos had finally broke up with Nadia. But at lunchtime when she slid her chair in next to Sybil's, it turned out Sybil already knew. "Nadia's suicidal," Sybil reported.

"How do you know, Sybil?" asked Ari, irritated.

"Oh, the usual way," said Sybil. "Tom-tom, grapevine, AT&T. Poor Nadia's prostrate—she's not even at school today. But if I were you, I'd be worried about Amanda." Sybil grinned. "Her position is that Cos is a criminal because he made Nadia cry. Melanie Russell saw Amanda in the hall, and she was muttering darkly about revenge."

"Well, I don't care what Amanda thinks." Ari stabbed her breaded veal cutlet. "But honestly! You'd think Nadia would have some pride. How can she let everybody know she's falling apart?"

"Cos is the only guy she ever loved. That's what she's telling everyone. She wants him back. Of course, Amanda keeps trying to persuade her that she doesn't want him back." Sybil shrugged. "She favors getting even."

Ari frowned. "Why doesn't Amanda mind her own business?"

"I don't know. But I'd watch my step, if I were you. Particularly at the Boo Ball. Amanda's a pretty average size and shape. She could be disguised as anybody!"

"The Boo Ball!" Ari exclaimed. "Oh, I forgot. Cos asked me to go with him."

"Oh," said Sybil.

"We can all three go together. It's all set," said Ari.

"Great," said Sybil sarcastically. "You and Cos making out in the front seat while I do my homework by flashlight in the back seat."

"We won't do that!"

"I think I know Cos a little better than you do," said Sybil. She cleared her throat. "Is Paul going?"

"Not with us," said Ari. "He can't stand Cos."

"Well—" began Sybil.

"He's got his eye on somebody to ask," said Ari quickly. "He told me so."

Sybil's face fell. "Not a red-haired girl with an interesting personality, huh?"

"A glamorous, empty-headed blonde with perfect fingernails," said Ari.

Sybil rested her chin on her fist. "Maybe I'll ask Nadia if she'd like to go with me. We could go as the public waterworks."

"Come with Cos and me," Ari urged her. "I promise it'll be fun."

When the twins got home that afternoon, a florist's black van was parked in front of the house. "Friendship Florist" was emblazoned in pink on its side. A man had the front door propped open with one foot while he slipped in the house with a vast arrangement of lilies and chrysanthemums. The twins followed him inside. The house dripped with flowers—the mantels and tables, even the table in the entry hall, were all banked with roses and lilies, and the faintly rotting scent of hothouse lilies filled the hallway.

A slender young man waltzed toward them and began talking very fast in Spanish to Carmel. Ari shrugged at Paul as streams of Spanish flowed over her head. To her relief, the young man switched to English. "You must be the niece and nephew," he said cheerfully. "I'm Ricardo, the caterer's man. You can go on with whatever it is that you do. We'll take care of absolutely everything." He smiled. "We are having a little problem obtaining fresh lobsters, but not to worry. We will cope. I have done Professor Montclair's parties before, and I absolutely understand that she must not be disturbed."

Ari exchanged a glance with Paul. Even the caterers knew about Aunt Gabrielle's beauty sleep, she thought. Didn't anybody else think it was weird for a grown woman to sleep all day and stay up all night?

As darkness fell, the twins heard car doors slamming, and the shrill hum of many voices downstairs. They went down at last to get something to eat and were astonished by the sheer crush of people. All the closely pressed bodies raised the temperature of the house by ten degrees. The white shirtfronts of the men and the white, powdered shoulders of the women gleamed in the dim light, and there was a discreet glitter of jewels. Paul finally managed to make his way to the buffet spread in the dining room. Cold lobster and crab claws dredged through a mayonnaise dip wasn't his usual supper, but he figured he would manage. He piled his plate high with tiny, fancy meringues and cheese pastries. He didn't see anything to drink but champagne, so he poured himself a glass. After he drank it, he still felt thirsty, so he poured himself another.

"You must be Gabrielle's nephew," said a red-faced man with a walrus moustache. He extended his hand. "Joe Donovan. Hear you're at St. Anselm's. My boy was there, too. He's at Dartmouth now. So have you given any thought to college yet?"

"Not yet," mumbled Paul. He polished off the crab legs, then grabbed a hard roll from the basket while Mr. Donovan talked about Dartmouth's football team. "Excuse me," Paul said after a few minutes. "I need to find my sister." It was slow going through the crowd. Several white-shirted men waylaid him and asked him how he liked Washington so far and whether he had given any thought to college. Paul did his best to be polite, but he began to wonder if Aunt Gabrielle had ordered these guys by the dozen from Central Casting. As far as he could make out, they generally worked for government agencies that were identified only by their initials.

He finally found Ari in the living room. She was standing by the fireplace, talking to two women who looked like a matched pair. Both were equally thin and both were in black. One wore a short slip dress and had her hair slicked back so tightly it looked enameled to her skull. Her eyebrows were plucked to a thin line over deeply shadowed gray eyes. The other wore full black crepe pants and had a thick fringe of blunt-cut hair that fell over one eye. It must have been a problem when she was driving, Paul thought, if she wanted to see who was coming at her from the left. Ari introduced the women as Gwendolyn and Tippi.

"About fifty people have asked me about my college plans," said Paul. "Is this what I've got to look forward to for the next two years?"

Gwendolyn tossed her hair out of her eye and gave him a warm smile. "I'm afraid so, kiddo. They can't think of anything else to say to someone your age. Haven't you ever wondered why people are called 'stuffed shirts'?"

"Not after tonight," said Paul.

Tippi giggled.

"Gwendolyn's a graphic artist," explained Ari. "Don't you think that's cool?"

Gwendolyn made a face. "It has its good points and bad points, like any job. Maybe you've seen our shop down by the harbor? It's the one with the dead body."

Paul stared at her.

"Not a real body," Tippi said with a smile. "It's for Halloween. Gwendolyn made a wild window display with a mannequin. It's terrifically realistic,

128

with blood and guts spilling out all over the place. Very gruesome."

"I worked from some illustrations in *Gray's Anatomy*. I was pretty satisfied with it," admitted Gwendolyn. "It took me all night, but I think people expect something spectacular from a graphic arts firm, don't you?"

Aunt Gabrielle appeared suddenly and threw her arms around Paul and Tippi. "Tippi and Gwendolyn! Two of my favorite people! I'm so glad you've met, darlings. Tippi and Gwen and I are the oldest of friends." Aunt Gabrielle smiled. "And both of them are so talented! Tippi doesn't like to say it, but she's a gifted dancer."

"You know I don't perform these days, Gabri," said Tippi. "I'm retired. But I do keep my hand in by teaching some night classes." Tippi perked up. "Oh, look, it's Derek!"

A cave-cheeked, blond man made his way over to them. He was wearing a black turtleneck. Something about him was familiar, but Paul couldn't put his finger on it. "Derek is the lead singer of Screaming Parsnips," Tippi explained. Paul supposed he had seen him on a poster somewhere.

After a flurry of air-kissing, the adults settled down to a discussion of Derek's recent trip to England. "Rain and gloom the entire time," Derek announced. "I went around everywhere muffled up."

"Neat-o!" cried Tippi. "Absolutely perfect."

It didn't seem perfect to Paul, but he had given up trying to figure Aunt Gabrielle's friends. He gulped down the last of his champagne and let the noise of the party wash over him. He noticed that there were two completely different sorts of people at the party—the stuffed-shirt government types and the skinny, offbeat types. Strange.

Ari touched his hand. "Are you all right, Paul?"

"Sure. I'm fine," he said, conscious of a certain difficulty forming consonants.

"You're sort of swaying," whispered Ari. "I think you'd better go upstairs and lie down until that champagne wears off."

Paul looked at his empty glass. Maybe Ari was right. His knees felt wobbly.

"I'll go with you," Ari said.

Aunt Gabrielle was talking animatedly to her friends when they left.

"I wish you'd lay off the booze," Ari said as she tucked Paul into bed. "What will I do if you become an alcoholic?"

"I only had a few glasses, Ari."

"Are you sure?" she asked.

"Well, I may have kind of lost track. The caterer's guys kept refilling my glass while I was talking to the old geezers about my not having any college plans."

Ari pulled the bedspread up under his chin and smiled at him. "Sleep tight."

But when she closed the door behind her, Paul didn't go to sleep. Instead he picked up the slip of paper by the bed. Susannah's phone number. He stared at it intently. The three was a sea-green color. The six was a pale blue. *The heck with it,* thought Paul. So he saw colors and numbers in color. It might be a little distracting, but it hadn't killed him yet. He picked up the phone and dialed Susannah's number.

When he heard her voice, his heart flipped over. "Susannah? This is Paul," he choked out.

"Hi," she said in a sweet, breathy voice.

He had tried to make chitchat with Susannah in class, but this was different. The usual conversation ploys, such as "So how's your sketchbook coming along," weren't any good to him in this instance. There was a long silence. Susannah didn't say anything, and Paul certainly couldn't think of anything to say. "Look, I was wondering if you'd like to go to the Boo Ball with me?" he said at last. "I hope you don't think this is too short notice or something."

"I'd like to go with you," she said.

"You would?" he asked. "Oh, good. Well, uh . . . see you in class."

After he hung up, Paul lay staring at the ceiling for a long time, worrying about what on earth he was going to say to Susannah for a whole evening at the Boo Ball. *Art,* he thought suddenly. He could talk to her about Michelangelo and people like that. It would be all right once he was actually with her, he assured himself, because then he could look at her and kiss those soft lips of hers. That was more what he had in mind. If he wanted intelligent conversation, he had Ari. He dozed off.

When he woke up, he was conscious that the house was quiet. The moving shadows in his room

131

were so creepy he switched on the light.

"Paul?" Ari pushed open her door and came in. She was in her nightgown. "Are you awake?"

"Now I am," he said irritably.

"Come in my room," she whispered. "I want to show you something."

"What's the big secret?" He threw back the covers and followed her into her room. Only the light that came from the door gave form to the bed and the fireplace in the shadows.

She tiptoed over to the window. "Look down there," she whispered. "Aunt Gabrielle is out on the terrace with a man."

"You're kidding me!" cried Paul.

"No—shh!"

He crept over to Ari's window and looked down onto the terrace below. The lights from the French doors in the dining room cast a fan of light onto the terrace. The view from the second floor made the figures below so foreshortened that he wasn't sure he would have recognized Aunt Gabrielle, but Ari had thrown her window open, and he heard Aunt Gabrielle's distinctive, musical voice. He couldn't make out what she was saying.

"That must be her boyfriend," hissed Ari.

Paul looked down. He could see the gleam of the man's white shirtfront and the roundness of his fleshy bald head. Suddenly he looked up and Paul drew back, but not before he saw a familiar face, strongly lit from one side, with a white walrus moustache. It was Joe Donovan, the man whose son had gone to St. Anselm's.

"Don't worry—they can't see us. We're in the shadows up here," whispered Ari. "Look, she's kissing his neck!"

Paul knew they shouldn't be watching, but he couldn't seem to help himself. He stared down and suddenly, to his horror, Mr. Donovan's head rolled to one side, and he slumped to the pavement. He lay on the bricks, his legs bent, his arms thrown out spread-eagle. "He passed out!" whispered Paul.

Aunt Gabrielle knelt beside him, her full shimmering skirt spread out around her in a circle. The French doors flew open, and two men hurried out and pulled Mr. Donovan to his feet. Paul was relieved to see that he didn't seem to be completely unconscious. He was able to hold his head up, at least, as they helped him inside.

The twins sat cross-legged on Ari's bed and stared at each other in wonder. "Jeez, talk about a passion pit," said Paul. "The guy actually fainted. If you ask me, he's too old for that kind of thing. He told me he's got a kid in college."

"I guess he must be divorced," said Ari doubtfully.

"Or he could still be married," said Paul. "He could have had a heart attack. You know, from the guilt."

Ari's door was ajar and a while later they heard the sharp tapping of Aunt Gabrielle's high heels coming up the stairs. The twins peeked out. "Has everybody gone home?" Ari called out.

Aunt Gabrielle turned and smiled at them. "Yes. But I'm afraid Derek and Tippi had to drive Joe home. He had too much to drink." Her mouth

133

screwed up in an expression of sudden distaste. "He smokes too much. He stinks of it and his circulation isn't what it ought to be." She pulled jeweled combs out of her upswept hair and shook her magnificent mane of black hair loose. Her face had a faint glow of warmth, as if she had just gotten back from jogging. "It was a lovely party, though, wasn't it?" she said with an absent smile. Her eyes were half-closed, as if she were dreaming. "I love the night when it's *plus noir qu'une mûre,*" she said softly. She blew them a kiss and went into her room, closing the door behind her.

Paul looked at Ari dubiously. "She's in an awfully good mood, considering some poor guy just passed out when she was kissing him."

Ari stared at her twin in silence.

"What's the matter?" Paul reached out to touch his sister. "Ari, are you okay?"

"Didn't you hear what she said?" whispered Ari.

"You know I don't follow it when she starts talking French," said Paul irritably. "Between Carmel spouting Spanish and Aunt Gabrielle showing off in French, half the time I don't know what is going on."

"Plus noir qu'une mûre," repeated Ari. "That's what she said. She said she loved the night when it was blacker than a blackberry."

Paul shrugged. "So?"

"Paul, that's exactly what the vampire said in the vampire diary!"

CHAPTER
TWELVE

A GRAYNESS AT THE WINDOW SHOWED THAT THE SUN was hovering at the verge of the horizon. A white face materialized before Ari's eyes, its skin taut over a handsome aquiline nose. Its dark eyes were bright and seemed to burn with an unearthly glow. Ari's stomach contracted with fear, and a scream welled up in her throat—she choked on her breath. The man's white skin looked as hard and glossy as the skin of a reptile, and his ears had a soft, feline point. His lips curled into a smile, and Ari saw his white fangs gleaming close before her. She was racked suddenly with nausea, and a low moan escaped her. The face drew back. If only she could make her frozen limbs move, she knew the horrible vision would vanish. With a painful effort, she reached her trembling arm toward the bedside lamp and clicked the light on. The fanged man froze a moment, his hand on the doorknob, his black-caped figure casting a distorted shadow in the corner. Then he turned swiftly, opened the door, and was gone. Ari stared after him, her mouth dry and her heart pounding. There had been a shadow on the wall! she realized with horror. A cold chill crept up her spine. None of her visions ever had shadows!

Ari sat bolt upright in bed. Her skin felt as if it had shrunk and her fingers were icy. She slid her feet to the cold floor and stood up, then ran over to the bedroom door and touched the knob. It was cold. Ice-cold. She felt a thud of relief. No warm hand had grasped that knob. The fanged man *had* been one of her visions. She ran to the connecting door between the bedrooms and threw it open. "Paul!" she cried.

He sat up. "Good grief, Ari." He glanced at the clock. "It's six thirty! What are you doing up already?"

She pulled back the covers and slid into bed with him, shivering. "Paul, you have weird dreams, right?"

"Yeah," he said cautiously. "I told you I did. I expect everybody does, sometimes."

"But do you . . . ever have them when you're awake?"

Paul swallowed. "Sometimes."

"What do you see?"

He thought of the fanged creatures in medieval dress. Somehow he couldn't bring himself to tell Ari about them. "Sometimes I see our father," he said hesitantly. "It happens just when I'm waking up."

Ari gazed at him wide-eyed. "What does he look like in your dream?"

"Sort of like me," said Paul simply.

Ari shivered. "I dream of fanged things," she said in a small voice. "Awful fanged things. This morning was the worst. I dreamed a fanged man was in my room. He was so real!"

"I sometimes have those dreams, too," said Paul. "But it's normal."

"Normal?" Ari gave a harsh laugh. "How can it be normal?"

"I looked it up when I was in the school library. There are these things called hypnagogic and hypnopompic images. Some people have them when they're waking up or going to sleep. It doesn't mean you're going crazy or anything."

Ari was silent for a moment. "Why didn't you tell me?"

"It was only a few days ago that I looked it up. Anyway, now you know."

"Paul," Ari darted an anxious look at her twin. She licked her dry lips. "When you see numbers, are they in color?"

He sucked in his breath sharply. "You see numbers in color, too?"

"Three is pink." She glanced at him shyly under her lashes. "Isn't that weird?"

"Yes." He grinned. "For me three is always seagreen." He felt as if a heavy weight had been rolled off his chest.

Ari took a deep breath. "It must be something hereditary," she said. "Like being born with an extra toe."

Ari felt her twin's hand in hers, and a surge of

sympathy coursed through their linked fingers, as still and quiet as the line of blue and green where ocean meets sky. Her heart beat in tune with his, a slow, quiet rhythm.

A spray of rain rattled against the windowpane. Dawn had come but it was a gray, wet dawn.

Suddenly Paul put his hands under Ari's arms and tossed her up. She laughed as he caught her. "Put me down!" she protested.

"I feel sorry for people who don't have a twin," he said, letting her slip down. "Don't you?"

It was almost time for school to start. Rain dripped with depressing regularity from the eaves of the school buildings. The courtyard formed by the three main classroom buildings smelled of wet earth and was clogged with sodden leaves. Two girls sat huddled together on a bench, listening to the mournful drip. "I was such an idiot," Nadia sobbed.

Amanda clenched her fists. "You're better off without him. What a jerk!"

"No, I'm not!" cried Nadia. "I love him!" She wiped her eyes. "And he loves me. I know he does. It's only that Ari's put a spell on him. Can't you see the way she looks at him?" Nadia shuddered. "Her teeth are pointy, like an animal's. How can he think she's pretty? She must have used magic. She's hypnotized him—I'm sure of it!"

"Look, you'd better pull yourself together before we go inside."

"No! I can't! And I don't even care!" wailed

Nadia. "If he feels sorry for me, maybe he'll come back to me!"

"You don't want him to come back to you because he feels sorry for you," protested Amanda, horrified.

"Oh, yes, I do!" cried Nadia. "I want to get him back any way I can."

"Think of the way he's treated you!" urged Amanda. "You should be furious! You should want to show him you don't care."

"But I do care," sniffled Nadia.

Amanda held out another tissue. "He's slime, Nadia. He's scum."

"How can he treat me this way?" cried Nadia, tears streaming down her cheeks. "All I've ever done is love him!"

Amanda's eyes narrowed. "If you could just get back at him, you'd feel so much better."

Cos sat next to Ari at lunch. Under the table, he had one hand possessively on her knee.

"It's nice to see you're finally keeping your elbows off the table, Cos," commented Mr. Fleming.

Cos flashed Ari a wicked grin.

"I wish Amanda would quit looking at me like that," he said. "It kills my appetite." He thrust a forkful of noodles into his mouth.

Ari glanced across the room. Sure enough, Amanda's dark eyes directed a look of malevolent hatred in their direction.

"I wonder what she's thinking," said Ari uneasily.

"Don't ask," groaned Cos. "She's probably plotting

murder. Did you hear about the time in second grade that she glued some poor turtle to a rock?"

"Actually, Sybil did tell me about that."

"It just goes to show you. The girl is capable of anything," said Cos. "Nadia used to be completely under her thumb. It was pathetic. She didn't have a single opinion of her own. I tried to show her that there was another way of looking at things than the way Amanda looked at them."

"Have you got your costume for the Boo Ball yet?" asked Ari. She was remembering Sybil's warning about the Halloween party. It would be easy for Amanda and Nadia to pull a trick on them there, when everyone was in disguise.

"I have got my costume." Cos smiled. "But I'm still not telling what it is. What about you?"

"Paul and I are going after school to get ours," said Ari.

Aunt Gabrielle had left a note on the dining room table for them, giving the address of a costumer and suggesting that they take a cab to his shop after school. "I hope it won't be too late for us to get something good," said Ari. "This is pretty short notice to be digging up a costume. Maybe all the good ones will be gone."

"You'd look great in anything," said Cos. "Have you thought about going as a belly dancer?"

"I'd freeze to death!" protested Ari.

"Don't worry," Cos said, leaning toward her and smiling. "I'll keep you warm."

*　　　*　　　*

The art class was doing a life study, and Susannah had volunteered to pose wearing a leotard. She could hardly have had a more electrifying effect on Paul if she had stripped bare. He sketched the graceful curve of her hip and thigh, but when he thought about how they were going to be in a dark car together on Friday night he could feel himself going warm all over.

"Are Ari and Cos going together these days?" Sandy asked, elaborately casual. He had sketched in an outline of Susannah's body and was working on carefully positioning eyes and ears on her oval head. Paul was astonished at his friend's inhuman detachment. Sandy was acting as if Susannah were merely an interesting arrangement of lines.

"What did you say, Sandy?" asked Paul. "Would you run that by me one more time?"

"Your sister, Ari," repeated Sandy. "What's the story between her and Cos?"

"Oh, him. He's going with Ari and Sybil to the Boo Ball."

"You mean Ari and Cos are just friends?" Sandy looked surprised.

Paul hesitated. "Cos is chasing after her," he said. "But, heck, we practically just got here. Ari has hardly had a chance to get to know anybody yet. She's still looking around."

"What's she going to wear to the Boo Ball?" asked Sandy.

"I don't know what we're going as yet," said Paul.

"You'll let me know what you decide on, won't you?"

"Sure," said Paul. He glanced down at his paper in astonishment. He had been drawing while he talked, more or less on automatic pilot, and he had almost finished. But the sketch didn't look exactly like Susannah. To his horror, Paul had unconsciously sketched in fangs. Quickly, with the heel of his hand, he smeared the charcoal before anyone could see.

Sandy glanced at Paul's sketch. "Jeez!" he said. "What happened? You've ruined the face."

"My hand slipped," said Paul in a flat voice. He was having trouble catching his breath. Vampires were lurking around every corner—in his dreams and in his waking life. There was no escape from them.

Later that afternoon, the cab dropped Paul and Ari off at a path that ran along the old C and O Canal. They could hear the water rushing in the nearby lift lock. Rainwater dripped damply from the trees onto the dark bronze bust of Chief Justice Douglas that stood on a plinth nearby. Small row houses had signs announcing their business—take-out pizza, law offices. Ari spotted the place they were looking for almost at once—"WILEY HOBAN, COSTUMER AND DESIGNER," said a wooden sign. The door had a glass window, but it was curtained with thin white material so they couldn't see inside the shop. The twins pushed the door open and a bell tinkled. At first, they saw

142

only the bolts of material that stood tall against the walls. Strings of glittering beads hung in one corner, and on the walls were jeweled crowns, felt hats, and rubbery masks—their expressions comically distorted by their hanging sagging on long nails.

A little man stepped out from behind a curtain at the back of the shop. He was gray and balding, with glasses that had slipped down on his nose. He was wearing a long white apron with a bib that was skewered with pins. "May I help you?" he inquired.

"We need costumes," said Paul. "I think you know our aunt, Gabrielle Montclair."

Mr. Hoban rubbed his hands together. "Oh, yes, I know Gabri very well indeed. She has an account here. Now what do you need?"

"We need something for a party next Friday night," said Ari.

The man blinked. "Next Friday! Dear me. Well, there's no time to design something new, then. You're welcome to step into the back and see what you can find from the stock I've got on hand."

The twins stepped behind the muslin curtain, and Ari sneezed. The dark room in the back of the shop was quite dusty. It contained department-store clothing racks. Each rack was heavy with costumes. Ari pulled out a glittery mermaid costume and held it up. It had a trailing quilted fish tail that could be a problem if she were dancing. Not to mention that the mermaid's thin, glittery bodysuit did not look exactly warm. "I want something warmer," said Ari, putting it back on the rack.

"Medieval is very warm," said Mr. Hoban promptly. "In those days, people lived in drafty castles." He began pulling out burgundy-colored velvet robes, wimples, and chains of jewels, but Ari didn't want to go to her first party with Cos dressed in the equivalent of a velvet bathrobe.

"I had in mind something more alluring," Ari said.

Mr. Hoban tossed the velvet robes aside and led her to a corner of the room where embroidered satin dresses hung in shiny plastic dry cleaner's bags. "Many of our ladies like a Marie Antoinette look. You're kind of small. Can you wear an eight or a ten? I don't carry anything smaller in this look."

Ari held the ball gown up to her and felt a flutter of excitement. An eight or a ten was what she usually wore. And unlike some of the women at Aunt Gabrielle's party, she had a figure. When she went in the dressing room and tried it on, the dress seemed to fit. It was obviously supposed to be snug. She stepped outside and pirouetted before her twin.

"Jeez," said Paul. "It's cut low enough! You'll probably bust out of it. If you cough, the sides will split."

"Oh, our seams are reinforced." Mr. Hoban smiled. "This is a very popular model. It comes with a powdered wig and a beauty patch complete with adhesive."

"I'll take it," said Ari.

"The jeweled mask is extra," he said.

"I'll take that, too," she said.

Paul settled on a bright-red demon outfit. He didn't want to risk some complicated costume falling in his eyes or tripping him up. The last thing he wanted was to look like an idiot in front of Susannah.

Mr. Hoban boxed up the costumes to go. The ball gown took a huge box, and Ari's wig was in its own very large hatbox. The demon costume slipped neatly into a Ziploc plastic bag. "I'll send the bill to the usual address on N Street," Mr. Hoban said, twirling his Rolodex.

Minutes later, the twins piled into a taxi. Ari couldn't see over the box in her lap. "This is going to be fun," she said.

A slow smile spread over Paul's face. "I hope so."

CHAPTER THIRTEEN

WHEN PAUL AND ARI WALKED DOWNSTAIRS, ARI caught a glimpse of herself in the mirror over the mantel in the living room. She saw a beautiful eighteenth-century lady in a tall, white powdered wig. The dress was very low-cut, and her breasts swelled above the tight embroidered satin.

Aunt Gabrielle clapped her hands in delight. "Utterly splendid!" she cried. "I love that little beauty patch by your eye!" She gave a low, throaty laugh. "You know, normally no one believes in restraint and self-control more than I do—I'm an absolute bore on the subject. But I do think that on Halloween one should . . . uh . . . let 'er rip."

Paul glanced at Ari. "I just hope it doesn't," he said.

Ari glared at him.

"I better get going," he said. "Susannah lives halfway across town."

"Drive carefully," said Aunt Gabrielle, looking anxious. "The streets are wet."

"Don't worry," said Paul. "I'm not about to put a dent in the new car." Aunt Gabrielle had arranged to have a little red Mazda delivered to the house for the twins, and they still hadn't gotten over the thrill of inhaling its new car smell.

After Paul left, Ari went in the living room where she could get a better look at herself in the mirror. The foaming white hair was quite dramatic with her dark eyebrows and lashes.

"You look beautiful," cried Aunt Gabrielle.

Ari felt a sudden catch in her throat. She wished that her mother could see her.

The doorbell rang. "That's your beau now," said Aunt Gabrielle. She pressed her cold cheek to Ari's affectionately. "I hope you have a wonderful time!"

"I will," said Ari, drawing away. She wished her aunt didn't have such white, clawlike hands. She ran to the door and threw it open. The blood drained from her face. A vampire stood on the stoop in a full black satin cape, his fangs pressing against his bottom lip. A tiny cry escaped Ari.

"Wow!" said Cos's voice. Then Ari recognized Cos, his face covered with thick white makeup. He was wearing wax fanged teeth over his own teeth and was staring at her as if struck speechless.

Ari flushed. Her costume was obviously a success. She regained her composure and hastily introduced Cos to Aunt Gabrielle. Cos tucked his fangs away in his pocket and bowed.

"Nice costume," purred Aunt Gabrielle. "Quite authentic-looking, if I may say so."

"Thanks," said Cos. "I wish we could stay and chat, but I'm double-parked."

Ari grabbed her jeweled mask off the table in the hall.

"Go, go!" cried Aunt Gabrielle, shooing them out.

Ari lifted her skirts as she moved carefully down the brick steps and the damp brick sidewalk to Cos's car. "Uh-oh," she said. "I don't think this eighteenth-century hair is made to fit in twentieth-century cars."

Cos opened the door. "Maybe if you sort of tilt your head back it'll be okay," he suggested.

Ari was barely able to squeeze in by scrunching down in her seat. Much of her hooped skirt had to be lifted up behind her and stuffed into the back seat of the car in order to give Cos room to drive.

"I wish I had a horse and carriage," said Cos, slamming his doors shut. "That dress wasn't made for a compact car." He slid in behind the wheel and cast a quick glance at Ari. "Sensational!"

"It is pretty," said Ari, looking down complacently at the gleaming satin.

"I wasn't talking about the dress," said Cos, doing a U-turn.

Sybil lived only a few blocks away. She came running out, wearing a sequined halter top and a glittery skirt with a jeweled yoke that began just below her belly button. Her earrings jingled as she got in the car. "I'm a belly dancer," Sybil announced, her teeth chattering.

"Aren't you freezing?" asked Ari.

"To death," said Sybil, wiggling into a navy-blue cardigan. "That's why my mom made me bring this sweater."

"You look terrific, Syb," said Cos. "I tried to get Ari to go as a belly dancer, but she had her own idea. Not that it wasn't a great idea." His fangs flashed white in the darkness.

The gym was dark and throbbing with loud music. Colored lights had been strung across the ceiling, and a strobe light rotated somewhere. Someone in a white bunny suit passed Ari. Under the colored lights, its ears turned blue then green before it disappeared into the crowd. Ari was confused by the shifting light.

"Stay close to me," Cos said to Ari. "I don't want to lose you." Immediately a farmer in a straw hat, plaid shirt, and overalls asked her to dance.

"Hey, I get the first dance," protested Cos, but the farmer whirled her away.

"What a dress!" said the farmer admiringly.

Ari recognized the voice of Paul's friend Sandy. "Thank you," she said, dimpling at him.

"Are you supposed to be somebody in particular?" asked Sandy.

"Marie Antoinette," she said.

"I hope you lose your head," he said, guiding her into a turn. He was wearing a black domino mask, but she could see that his neck was turning crimson. "Figuratively, I mean," he added.

"I thought that was what you meant," she said.

"I don't know why I said that," Sandy said. "I never make smart remarks. That's because I'm not any good at it. I just fall all over myself afterwards and end up looking stupid."

"I think you're doing fine," said Ari, smiling at him.

The vampire stepped into the gym and glanced up at the colored lights. The strobe light threw a band of pink over his white face. No one could tell who was human and who wasn't with this lighting, he thought with satisfaction. He spotted a heavily padded Humpty Dumpty moving awkwardly toward the punch bowl, his little blue hat wobbling. A skinny, red-haired belly dancer was doing a comical undulating dance with a boy who was wearing tight britches and a sweeping plumed hat. The vampire smiled. He loved Halloween! A celebration of rich diversity. And a perfect night for vampires. Even if someone looked at him closely, they would only compliment him on the artfulness of his costume. The vampire chuckled to himself as he looked around.

Suddenly he spotted Ari. Her wig swayed as she danced with the boy whose straw hat was pushed back on his head. Her lovely face was first green then blue as they danced under the colored lights. The moving light of the strobe made her seem ghostly, spiritlike. He pressed through the crowd until he reached them and tapped the farm boy on the shoulder.

"May I cut in?" he asked.

The boy looked at him, confused. Then the music stopped momentarily, and the boy dropped his arms to his side. "Oh," he said, glancing around at the vampire. "I guess you want to dance with the guy that brought you." He backed away from Ari, looking embarrassed.

"May I have the next dance?" asked the vampire in a silky voice.

"You aren't Cos!" cried Ari.

"No," said the vampire. "I'm not."

Ari's eyes opened wide. In the shifting light, she thought she recognized the face from her vision—the tightly drawn white skin and aquiline nose, the dark, glittering eyes of her nightmare.

"But can't we dance anyway?" suggested the vampire, his voice sweet. He reached out and she felt his cool hand on the back of her neck. She tingled from head to toe and felt vaguely sick as he took her in his arms and guided her into a slow two-step. Her head felt fuzzy and she was having trouble thinking clearly. The figures around them seemed to fade and grow dim.

"Tell me about yourself," he said softly.

Ari squirmed and tried to wriggle free from his grasp. She hated his eyes, like cat's eyes, staring into hers. A chill shook her. The achingly familiar feeling of being watched by alien eyes swept over her. She wanted to scream and break away from him, but she felt powerless, as if she were trapped in a dream. Her feet moved mechanically.

"I said, 'Tell me about yourself,'" said the man. His voice had taken on an edge. "Your thoughts,

151

your secrets. You heard me. Do as I say."

Ari's eyes widened and her mouth fell open. With a sickeningly painful effort of will, she froze. "N—no!" she exploded suddenly. A couple dancing nearby stared at her.

The man's eyes grew red with anger, and his grip on her loosened. Ari turned suddenly and stumbled through the crowd of dancers. She heard the vampire's muttered "Damn!" as she escaped.

Ari ran blindly toward the door. Suddenly she ran against a black-caped figure. He turned to face her, and his white face blurred as she gasped and recoiled from him.

"Ari? What's wrong?" Cos caught her under the arms as she sagged.

"Oh, Cos, it's you! I'm scared," she sobbed. She leaned her head on his chest. Her stomach heaved.

Cos's eyes darkened. "Did Sandy—?"

"No!" Ari choked out. "Sandy didn't scare me. It was this . . . this other vampire. I thought it was you, and then when I saw him up close I realized that he wasn't!" She thought with horror of her dance with the strange vampire. The will to resist had seemed to leak out of her fingertips; for a minute she had felt as if she had been a brainless mechanical doll. What had happened to her? She choked on a sob.

"Calm down," said Cos softly. "It's okay. I'm right here." He put his arm around her, and she felt herself grow calm. Cos's solidity and warmth were what she needed to steady her. The uncanny resemblance of the strange vampire to her vision had stunned her for a moment, that was all, she decided. She wouldn't think about it anymore.

"I won't let him scare you again," said Cos. "Come on, let's get some punch, huh?"

Paul had found a place a little set off from the party to talk to Susannah. In one corner of the gym, a long curtain of synthetic cobwebs had been tacked to the ceiling and pulled down to the floorboard in front of the bale of hay. Through the long strip of gauzy cobweb, the colored lights looked pastel and fuzzy. Susannah was leaning back against a bale of hay. Her blue pillbox hat trailed chiffon veils that caught a little on the straw, and her full-legged chiffon harem pants had a spray of hayseed stuck to them. Her midriff, Paul thought, looking down at her, was a work of art. He wanted to touch the faint tracery of her ribs and the shadowy indentation of her navel. He wanted to press her against the hay as he kissed her. But he sensed this was not the right time. She was talking about her second-grade teacher, giving him her life story.

"I was always the tallest one in the class," said Susannah earnestly. "They put me on the back row when they took the class picture. Pretty soon my mom couldn't even find Mary Jane shoes in my size, and I had to wear these awful grown-up shoes. I felt so tall I was afraid my head was going to break right through the roof one day. It was this morbid fear I had."

"I think you're a wonderful height," said Paul.

Susannah smiled. "Well, now I can appreciate

being tall," she said complacently. "I wouldn't want to be a little mouse of a thing like Nadia. But back then I was only seven and it was tough looking so grown-up. People expected more of me. They'd forget I was only seven. And then—"

Paul's mind wandered. He wondered if girls wore underwear under those skimpy costumes. Ari, he had noticed, always wore underwear, even if it was just a tiny scrap of filmy material not worth talking about. It must be some kind of superstition with girls.

"Wasn't that horrible of her?" Susannah looked at him expectantly, her eyes moist.

"Terrible," said Paul at once. "Very insensitive."

"It really traumatized me," said Susannah earnestly. "After that, I decided I wanted to be a teacher, because I would never, never make a crack like that to a sensitive little girl. I think teachers should always be careful of children's feelings, don't you?"

"Oh, definitely," said Paul, his eyes burning. "That's very, very important." And as he said it, suddenly he believed it. It seemed horrible to him that some teacher had hurt Susannah's feelings when she was in the second grade. He was inches from pressing Susannah against the hay to kiss her. The bristles of hay bit into his knee through the cloth of his costume and made his palm itch as he leaned over her.

Susannah smiled dreamily. "I knew you were different from the guys around here," she said, "the same old boring guys I grew up with. There was something about you."

His face drew close to hers. He could feel her warm breath.

"I love your teeth," Susannah said.

Paul blinked, thrown off his stride. "My teeth?"

She reached a forefinger into his open mouth and touched them. She giggled. "Your pointy teeth! They're sort of animal-like, you know? Dangerous."

Paul figured that was his cue. Supporting his weight on his hand, he pressed his lips to hers. He was so close to her that he could feel her warmth and the beating of her heart.

"Paul!" she cried, squirming under him.

He drew away and swallowed hard. He was having trouble thinking straight.

"There are chaperones all over the place!" cried Susannah.

Paul glanced over his shoulder and was relieved to see no teacher bearing down on them. "Let's go outside, then," he suggested.

Susannah hugged herself and shivered. "Outside! Are you kidding? I'd freeze."

Paul sighed. Susannah's skimpy costume, though pretty, was impractical.

Susannah struggled up from the stacked bales. Bits of hay clung to her chiffon scarf. "Let's dance," she said. "Come on." She tugged at him until he reluctantly trailed after her to the middle of the gym floor, and they joined the dancers.

Paul wondered how Ari was getting along. He had been concentrating so much on Susannah that he hadn't seen his twin all evening.

*   *   *

"It's hot enough in here, isn't it?" said Cos.

Ari was trying to push the horrible memory of her dance with the strange vampire out of her mind, and she scarcely heard him. Already her mind was foggy on the details of what he had said and what she had said. She didn't even care. It was bad enough to recall that feeling of being drained of her strength.

Cos unfastened his cape and draped it over one arm. "Has my makeup started to run?" He fingered his jaw uneasily. "I bet I'm melting."

She gulped down the last of her punch and shook her head. "You're fine. The makeup must be waterproof."

Cos put his arm around her. "Jeez, get a load of that costume," he said, and she felt him shiver. "Isn't that sick?"

Ari turned to see a girl in a black leotard carrying a tall aluminum ax. A loose black hood fell to her shoulders, concealing her head completely.

"Who's she supposed to be?" asked Ari, relieved that her voice sounded normal.

"The public executioner," said Cos. "Old-time executioners always wore hoods like that so nobody could see who they were. I'm surprised she didn't tuck a severed head under her arm for that authentic touch."

"It would be hard to dance with a head under one arm and the ax in the other," Ari pointed out.

The hooded head swiveled suddenly and looked straight at them. Ari could see the girl's

156

gleaming eyes peeking out at them from two holes in the black hood.

Cos squeezed Ari. "Watch her walk," he said in a low voice. "It's Amanda."

Ari watched the girl dressed in black walk away from them. There was something familiar about her long-legged stride.

"I hope she's not trying to send me a message with that executioner's costume," said Cos.

"Lots of people wear gruesome costumes on Halloween," she said. "After all, you came as Dracula, didn't you?"

"That's different," said Cos. "Everybody knows vampires aren't for real."

Ari blinked. She wasn't so sure anymore. "Nobody gets executed with axes anymore, either," she said in a faint voice. "Not in this country, anyway."

"I just wish I knew what Amanda was up to," said Cos. "She's making me nervous."

Ari gazed at the costumed figures on the crowded dance floor. She wished she could see the unknown vampire. She wanted to prove to herself that he was only a student and not the vampire from her dreams. Maybe Cos would recognize him and tell her who he was. She caught a glimpse of Paul in the red devil's costume. He whirled by them with Susannah in his arms, and her chiffon scarves wafted behind her in fluid swirls. A boy in a zebra-striped leotard poured himself some punch. His hair was brushed up into a Mohawk-style imitation of a zebra's mane. But Ari saw no

157

sign of the vampire who had frightened her. Since she'd come to St. Anselm's, she'd thought on several occasions that she recognized kids from her old school, only to realize the next moment that she was mistaken. Her mind insisted on trying to find familiar faces. Perhaps she only thought she recognized the vampire face from her dream, she told herself. The light had been confusing. It was another trick her mind was playing on her.

Cos handed her another glass of punch, and Ari smiled. As long as she was with Cos, she thought, the world was reliable and solid. But when she looked out at the dancers on the gym floor in the unearthly light, uncertainty swept over her, and the ground of reality seemed to shift under her feet. A Cyclops with a rubbery, wrinkled face moved by them, dancing with a dragonfly girl. The girl's shimmering gossamer wings were first pink then green, and her black antennae bobbed as she danced. The Cyclops's large bloodshot eye leered over her shoulder at Ari. She put down her punch, untouched. "Let's dance," she suggested abruptly. Somehow she had to shake the black mood that had fallen over her.

As Ari and Cos danced, the flashing light and the moving costumed figures around them jiggled and jerked like the reel of an old movie. The beat was fast and the heavy satin of Ari's skirt bounced. She grew hot and the colors she saw seemed blurred. Suddenly Cos's white face and fangs began to look like one of the creatures from her nightmare, and she gasped. She closed her eyes.

No! she reminded herself. It was Cos she was dancing with. She felt safe with him. He was nothing like the horrible vampire she had met moments before. But the strange vampire's face floated before her eyes and got confused in her mind with Cos's. Frantically, she danced faster until her chest was gleaming with sweat. The music changed suddenly, and Cos drew close to her, folding his arms around her.

"Mmmph," he said, smiling. "You are the greatest." He kissed the tiny black beauty spot glued at the corner of her eye, laughed, then kissed her again. Ari closed her eyes and sighed. With Cos's arms around her, she knew she was safe.

Loud music poured out of the doors as Paul and Susannah came out. Chiffon scarves floated behind Susannah as they moved down the hall. "We could go get something to eat," Paul suggested.

Susannah laughed. "Paul, I can't go anywhere dressed like this!"

"We could get take-out somewhere," said Paul urgently. "We could park outside the pizza place with the car heater on." Paul could hear his own and Susannah's footsteps echoing in the empty hallway. He had the uneasy feeling someone was watching them. It was as if he felt a gaze pressing against his shoulder blades. He was about to open the door and step outside, but he couldn't stop himself from turning suddenly and looking back. A blurry white shape moved over the open door.

Paul refocused his gaze and got a better look. The bunny rabbit he had seen earlier was standing behind one of the open gym doors. For some reason it looked oddly tall. Too tall. Paul blinked a second at the white shape behind the door, its ears bobbing slightly. What was that bunny rabbit doing hiding behind the door? he wondered. And why was it so tall?

"Oh, okay." Susannah's face turned up to his confidingly. "I guess we could park at the pizza place."

Paul wasn't listening. He suddenly had realized that the bunny must be Nadia. She was standing on a ladder. What on earth was she doing?

At that moment, a shadowy figure clad in black with a long satin cape emerged from the gym. For a second, Paul thought it was Cos. Then he realized the vampire was taller than Cos, and somehow he moved differently. Paul couldn't see very well and caught only a glimpse of a pale face and white hands.

Then a sudden movement out of the corner of his eye caught his attention, and he was startled to see a cloud of white envelop the vampire's head.

In slow motion as if it were a dream, Paul saw that Nadia, her white bunny ears bobbing, was leaning over the open door, holding an upturned plastic bucket. The vampire below her was white with flour, his cloak streaked and dripping with a flour-water paste. His white face turned up to look at Nadia, and Paul saw her wobble dangerously on her ladder.

A chill shot up Paul's spine, and he unconsciously gave Susannah a little push. "Let's get out of here," he said urgently. "Quick."

"I'm going as fast as I can!" she said. "What's the rush?" She turned as if to look, but Paul pushed open the door and hurried her outside. A blast of cold air hit him in the face. His blood was pulsing so hotly the night air could not chill him. It was none of his business what the rabbit was up to, he thought, and his instinct was to get away before all hell broke loose. He put his arm around Susannah and held her tightly as they ran.

A minute later Nadia ran sobbing out into the cold air. Her throat hurt and her ankle throbbed. She had to get away! Suddenly she collapsed on the sidewalk, scraping her palms.

"Nadia!" Amanda's face loomed over her, her eyes alarmed. "What's wrong? Are you all right? Can you get up?" Nadia felt her friend's strong hands lifting her as she struggled to her feet.

"I hurt my ankle," she sobbed.

"Can you put your weight on it?" asked Amanda.

Nadia tested it, wincing. "Yes, but it hurts a lot."

"It isn't broken, then. It's probably only sprained," said Amanda. "You shouldn't have taken off all of a sudden like that. What happened?"

"The vampire wasn't Cos, Amanda!" Nadia screamed. "Didn't you see? It wasn't him! It was a real vampire! A real one!"

Amanda took off her black hood and tucked it

into her waistband. Her sweaty hair clung to her scalp. "It was just some other guy in a vampire costume, Nadia," she said soothingly. "It's too bad we didn't realize there were two of them. We got flour and water all over some kid we don't even know."

"No!" Nadia shivered. "It wasn't a kid, Amanda. His face was so smooth, and he had eyes like coals. Burning eyes! You couldn't see him the way I could." She shuddered. "He was only pretending to be a kid! It was a real vampire!"

"We need to get you home," Amanda said, uncomfortably. "You've had a scare, but you'll feel better once you calm down."

"You don't believe me!" Nadia cried.

"We should get an Ace bandage on that ankle of yours," said Amanda.

"Do you think you're smarter than all the peasants in my grandmother's village?" cried Nadia. "They knew all about vampires. Vampires lie in wait for innocent people and suck their blood."

"Superstition," said Amanda shortly.

Testing her ankle, Nadia hobbled a few steps. "Maybe I used to think that, too," she admitted, shivering, "but now I see I was wrong. When that vampire looked at me, I was afraid he was going to pull me toward him with his eyes."

Amanda shrugged. "You got away from him, didn't you?"

"You don't believe me, do you?" cried Nadia.

Amanda put her hands on her friend's shoulders and studied her face closely. "You haven't been doing drugs, have you, Nadia?"

"No!" cried Nadia, twisting away from her. "This is real! It's not all in my mind."

"I didn't say it was all in your mind," Amanda said. "You're just . . . the sensitive type."

A sigh escaped Nadia. There was no use arguing, she thought. Amanda was incapable of understanding anything more supernatural than a soccer match.

"Trying to dump that flour on Cos was a stupid idea," Amanda said guiltily. "If I'd known how upset you were going to get, I never would have suggested it."

Nadia got in her car.

"Are you okay to drive?" asked Amanda.

"I'm fine," said Nadia.

"I'll give you a call tomorrow and see how you're feeling," said Amanda.

"Okay," said Nadia listlessly. She put the car in reverse and stepped firmly on the accelerator. Maybe Amanda would believe her, she thought grimly, once kids began to die.

CHAPTER
FOURTEEN

WHEN ARI WOKE UP THE NEXT MORNING, SHE stretched luxuriously. She felt snug and content. No fanged creatures were rummaging in her clothes, and she had almost forgotten the strange vampire at the dance.

Her embroidered satin ball gown hung on a hanger hooked over the door of the tall wardrobe. Her powdered wig, a mountain of white curls, was on a chair beside it, and the petticoat with its hoops collapsed sat untidily in a corner. She remembered Cos's lingering goodnight kiss as they stood shivering on the front stoop and smiled. Then she slipped into jeans and a shirt and knocked on the connecting door.

When Paul opened the door, to her surprise, he was already dressed. Usually she heard him moving around and showering in the morning. She must have slept very soundly.

"I thought you'd never wake up," he said. "Let's go down and get some breakfast."

It was understood that neither of them wanted to go downstairs alone in Aunt Gabrielle's gloomy house. Ari glanced uneasily at the crow and its black mirror as they passed Aunt Gabrielle's door. Breathing fast, the twins fled from the crow's glassy gaze and hurried down the dark staircase.

"Jeez," said Paul, feelingly, "if I owned this place, I'd slap some white paint over the paneling. It gives me the creeps."

It was brighter downstairs. Sunlight poured in the big French doors of the dining room and made the brass gong beside the door glow.

In the kitchen, there was no sign of Carmel since it was Saturday. Paul poured himself some cold milk, then rummaged around until he found coffee cake in the fridge. "You want yours heated up?" he asked, his mouth full.

"Wait a minute," said Ari. Frowning, she went back to the narrow hallway that served the kitchen and pantries. "Paul, come back here!"

He found her kneeling in the service hallway. Her fingers trailed across the white smear that lightened the floor just outside the kitchen. "I thought the floor looked funny." Ari frowned. "I figured I'd better come back and take a second look."

"Looks like something was spilled," said Paul, "and Carmel didn't do such a hot job of cleaning it up."

Ari glanced up at her twin. "It's flour. I can feel that it's powdery."

Paul stared uneasily at the stain. "Flour," he repeated dully.

Ari stood up and went back into the kitchen without saying a word and poured herself some milk. She stared absently at the glass. "Paul, what time did you leave the party last night?"

"Oh, I don't know. About midnight or one. Susannah and I went and got a bite to eat afterwards." He avoided her eyes.

"You didn't see what happened when somebody dumped the bucket of flour?"

"I saw the whole thing," Paul admitted. "It was Nadia. I saw her standing on a ladder behind the gym door in that bunny suit of hers. I even saw her dump it. I think she must have been after Cos, because whoever she dumped it on was dressed like a vampire."

"Listen!" Ari's breath came quickly. "There *was* a strange vampire at the dance last night. He asked me to dance and I'd never seen him before."

Paul shook his head. "It's not like you know everybody, though, Ari."

"He was strange," Ari said in a low voice. "He looked like one of the vampires I saw in those dreams I have. You know, the hypnagogic or hypnopompic stuff."

"How could he?" said Paul firmly. "Those are just dreams."

"I'm just telling you, he did," said Ari. The memory of her dance with the vampire made her sick, and she had to close her eyes. "I bet he was the one that got the flour all over him."

Suddenly she got up. "I'm going to go over to Sybil's house," she said. "If the buckets fell on an actual kid, Sybil may know who it was by now."

Paul squirmed. "Well, you know those buckets didn't fall on a dream, Ari. It's impossible."

"We'll see," said Ari stubbornly. "Sybil will know."

"Do you have to go over there?" Paul's face fell. "Why don't you just ask her on the phone? I don't want to be stuck here in the house all by myself."

"Come with me, then," said Ari.

"You know I can't. Sybil'd be chasing me with a butterfly net."

"Why don't you go visit Susannah, then?"

"I saw Susannah last night," Paul said sullenly.

"I don't know why you can't go out with Sybil. She's a really interesting, high-energy sort of person."

"Okay, if you pick out my girlfriends, then I get to pick out your boyfriends. Fair enough?" Paul smiled.

"I was only making a suggestion. I wouldn't think of interfering in your love life."

Paul snorted. "Yeah. I bet you wouldn't."

Ari dialed Sybil on the kitchen phone. When she hung up, Paul picked at his coffee cake, looking depressed.

"You sure you won't come with me?" Ari wheedled. "Sybil would love to have you."

"I bet she would," said Paul.

Ari took a quick swig of milk. "Gotta go," she said. "I told her I'd be right over." She looked at her twin seriously. "If you won't come with me, I

167

wish you'd go to the mall or something, Paul. I don't want you to be here by yourself."

Paul looked up. "Don't worry," he said dryly. "Auntie Gabrielle will keep me company."

"Very funny," said Ari. "You know she never shows her face until it gets dark. Besides . . ." she hesitated, "I'm not sure how much I trust her."

Paul shrugged uncomfortably.

Ari planted a forefinger on Paul's chest. "Just suppose," she said, "that the flour got dumped last night on the mystery vampire! And just suppose that smear of flour on the floor in the hall means he came sneaking into Aunt Gabrielle's study through the garden and then across the hall and up the back stairway right to her bedroom!"

"Are you saying the mystery vampire was Aunt Gabrielle?" Paul was puzzled.

"No!" said Ari. "I saw him close up. He's got a kind of beaky nose. He didn't look a bit like Aunt Gabrielle."

Paul's eyes narrowed. "Then are you trying to tell me you think Aunt Gabrielle's got something going with some guy from our school?"

Ari seemed struck by this thought. "That's an idea! I hadn't even thought of that. Maybe it was a teacher dressed up like a vampire!"

"I hope he was cuter than that stuffed shirt she was making out with at the party," said Paul.

"I am going over to see Sybil," said Ari, "and I wish you would get out of the house until we find out what's going on."

Paul saluted. "Aye, aye, sir. Maybe I'll go over to Sandy's house."

Paul dropped Ari off at the corner of Twenty-ninth and Dunbarton. From there she could see Sybil's house down the block. It was a brick house rather like Aunt Gabrielle's with a Federal-style front door and black shutters. But the house on the corner had a picket fence and a front yard, an unusual feature in Georgetown, where most houses were built up to the street and jammed up close to their neighbors. The house was almost hidden by a huge tree, its leaves flaming yellow, which helped conceal a generous porch in the old-fashioned style. As Ari passed it, she was startled when a lady pushed opened the gate. She wore a broad, stiff, old-fashioned skirt, and she seemed to have appeared from nowhere with a sudden rustle of her crinoline petticoats.

Ari looked curiously after the woman. Someone coming home late from a Halloween party, she decided, dressed in Civil War style. The woman had a tiny waist but plump arms, bare to the cool autumn air. Her glossy hair was trained in unbecoming sausage curls close to the head at either temple. The woman paused at the corner of Dunbarton and Twenty-ninth, as if she hoped to hail a cab. Ari noticed with a start that she could see the fire hydrant right through the woman's skirt. Suddenly the woman vanished. Ari's heart was pounding hard, and she stumbled on the uneven brick of the sidewalk as she hurried to Sybil's house and knocked on the door.

Sybil flung open the door. "Ari! What's wrong? You're white as a ghost."

"I need to sit down," said Ari. She suited the word to the deed by sitting down at once on the bottom step of the stairs. The woman she had just seen could not be a hypnogogic or hypnopompic vision, she realized, because she was wide awake. Maybe dream images were starting to invade her waking hours. The vampire at the party could have been a dream image come to life, too. "Sybil, who lives in the house on the corner?" she gasped.

Sybil giggled. "A ghost! I'm serious. That house is on all the tours. My dad could tell you all about who built it and everything—it's some important historical place—but all I remember is that's where the ghost lives. Supposedly she came to lunch sometime in the last century and never went home."

"I saw her," said Ari.

"You didn't!" cried Sybil. "It's so unfair! I've lived on this block for ten years, and I've never seen her even once."

"But other people have seen her?" asked Ari anxiously. If other people had seen the ghost, maybe she wasn't going crazy after all.

"Well, it's not like the Loch Ness monster where people come up with photographs they sell to the *National Enquirer,*" said Sybil. "It's more like a legend. I don't personally know anybody who's seen her except you."

"Well, I saw something," said Ari. "It could have been somebody left over from a Halloween party except that her skirt was—" Ari wrinkled her nose "—transparent. I could see the fire hydrant right through her!"

Sybil's high, arched eyebrows rose. "Have you ever tried a Ouija board, Ari? I bet you'd be awfully good at it."

A woman with silver-frosted hair stepped into the foyer. "You must be Ari," she said warmly. She extended her hand.

Ari shook hands. "That's what everyone calls me," she said. "But Anne-Marie Montclair is my real name."

Ari felt Mrs. Barron's hand go rigid. The smile froze on her face. "Is your family from around here?" Mrs. Barron asked, her voice quavering.

Ari wondered what on earth was going on; Mrs. Barron seemed stunned by Ari's name. "My father's family is from around here," she said. "But my aunt Gabrielle is the only one of the Montclairs I know. My brother and I grew up in New Orleans."

"Oh," said Mrs. Barron. She backed out of the foyer. "Nice meeting you," she said faintly.

Sybil and Ari looked at each other a minute, and Sybil shrugged. "Search me," Sybil said flatly. "Sometimes she acts kinda weird. Want to go up to my room?"

The girls ran upstairs. Sybil's house was very different from Aunt Gabrielle's. The floor plan was similar, but the Barrons' house was full of light, air, and fresh flowers. Sybil's bedroom was a bower of white lace, with white lace pillows and billowing curtains. "You can see why I don't have many people over," Sybil said. "I tried to get Mom to let me redecorate with black walls and a tweed bedspread, but she got hysterical. She's sort of high-strung."

"I can see that," said Ari. "Does she always freak out when you introduce your friends?"

"Oh, no! She's always trying to get me to bring my friends home. 'Where are your friends?' she keeps saying. Mom wishes I were popular like she was."

"But people like you, Sybil," protested Ari. "I like you. Cos likes you."

"I don't mean that kind of popular. I mean popular like 'Homecoming Queen' and 'Sweetheart of the Key Club.' Mom doesn't quite catch on that people don't do that stuff anymore. I'm a disappointment to her. I'm surprised she froze up on you like that, though. Usually she's charming. Charming is what she does for a living. It's very helpful when she's entertaining my dad's law clients."

"Maybe it's me," said Ari, sitting down on the bed. "Maybe she simply doesn't like me."

"No," said Sybil. "I think it's your name. She was fine until she heard your name. I've got it! I'll bet she once had an affair with your dad! How about that!" She grinned.

"Very funny," said Ari uneasily. Why did her father's name have to keep turning up?

172

"They could have had a thing going back to when they were in high school," insisted Sybil. "They must be about the same age. You did say your dad's family is from around here."

Ari nodded. "My dad actually went to St. Anselm's. Isn't that funny?"

"And my mom went to the St. Anne's School for Girls, which used to be right next door." Sybil licked her lips. "I think we're onto something. They must have known each other. Of course, that was back before St. Anselm's went coed, but I think a lot of the activities between the girls' and the boys' schools were coordinated. This is so neat!" Sybil bounced on the bed. "Just think, Ari, if it had worked out a little differently we could have been sisters."

"If it had worked out between your dad and my mom, then neither of us would exist," Ari said flatly. "You're jumping to a lot of conclusions. Maybe your mother doesn't like me because she hates Aunt Gabrielle or because she doesn't like my looks."

"You are such a spoilsport," said Sybil. "I say we try to find out. Let's look for evidence." Sybil tapped her fingernail on her braces thoughtfully. "We could ask my mother," she suggested.

"*I'm* not going to ask her," said Ari. "You ask her."

"But she might lie," said Sybil promptly, "so that wouldn't prove anything. Wait a minute! I've got it. My mom's old photo albums! Wait here a minute."

Sybil crept out of the room with ostentatious stealth, like a villain in an old melodrama. It was only after she left the room that Ari remembered she hadn't had a chance to ask Sybil what she had come over to ask her. That bucket of flour—who had it landed on?

A few minutes later, Sybil returned staggering under the weight of several heavy photo albums. "I think we're onto something," she panted. "I've already taken a peek."

"You're kidding me!" Ari felt herself go cold. "You mean my father is in your mom's old photo albums?"

"Richard Montclair?" smirked Sybil. "He's there, all right."

"Give me those!" cried Ari. Her hands trembled as she took the album. "I don't even know what he looks like," she said. "When my parents split, Paul and I were too little to remember."

"Isn't this exciting!" cried Sybil. "Flip over to the picture of the third form's string quartet. That's where I spotted the name."

Sybil flipped ahead until she came to a large glossy that showed four serious teenagers. The three boys had buzz cuts and looked like recent inductees into the Army. The girl's hair was in a stiff flip. She wore a full skirt and her ankles were demurely crossed. The picture was labeled "Richard Montclair, Tom Cannon, Averill Harrison, Self."

"That's my mom," said Sybil. "The one called 'self.'"

The young Mrs. Barron was staring at the serious dark-haired boy with the cello. He looked soft with baby fat, almost pretty, but Ari thought she could make out a slight resemblance to Paul.

"Flip ahead," Sybil urged her. "I think they must have been pretty chummy."

Several pages on was another large glossy, this time a prom picture. Mrs. Barron, wearing a strapless tulle evening dress with rows of ruffles and with a corsage of carnations strapped to her wrist, was beaming at the camera. Standing next to her was a tall, dark boy with high cheekbones. He was dressed in patent leather shoes, a black jacket with satin lapels, and a black bow tie. "Richard Montclair and Self," the picture was labeled carefully. "Spring Formal."

"Isn't that weird!" Sybil breathed. "Your mother and my dad went to the prom together. Unbelievable!"

Ari stared at the picture for some time as if willing the photograph to give up the secret of what her father was like. But all she saw was a stiffly self-conscious teenager who vaguely resembled her brother. What had she expected? she wondered.

"Keep looking," said Sybil. "Maybe we'll find some more pictures."

Ari turned the page. Anyone would have imagined Richard Montclair was a member of Sybil's family, thought Ari; he was on almost every page of the photo album. Soon "Richard Montclair" was shortened simply to "Richard." Over the course of two albums, Ari watched Richard's baby fat disap-

175

pear. His nose and cheekbones grew more pronounced, and his smile grew confident and charming. In swim trunks he balanced on one foot, laughing, on an anonymous boat dock. In heavy makeup with a wig he was "Richard as Macbeth." Then came a Halloween picture with him dressed as Dracula. Ari stared mesmerized at the Instamatic snapshot—the aquiline nose under the white makeup, the dark eyes. Though the features were softer, he looked disturbingly like the vampire of her bad dream, the one who had terrified her at the Boo Ball. Ari could feel that her palms were damp as she clenched and unclenched her fists. "Sybil, who did that bucket of flour fall on last night?"

"That's the funniest thing!" said Sybil. "Nobody seems to know. I must have called fifty people and nobody's got a clue. Six people told me it was Cos, but we know for sure it wasn't him."

"Paul saw the whole thing. Nadia dumped the flour," said Ari.

"That would make sense," said Sybil promptly. "Since Cos broke up with her, I've been halfway expecting she'd do something crazy like this, but if it was her, you can bet Amanda was helping her. Nadia doesn't have the nerve to do it by herself. You'd think they'd be trying to get Cos, but they must have messed up somehow."

"I think I know how. I think they got another vampire instead. I have this weird feeling," Ari said, "that my father was at the party dressed like Dracula. He asked me to dance."

Sybil looked at her blankly. "And you didn't even

176

recognize him? Oh, I forgot. You didn't know what he looked like, so how could you recognize him?"

"Can I borrow one of these pictures, Sybil?" asked Ari grimly. "I want to show Paul what our dad looks like."

"Sure," said Sybil. "Which one?"

Ari chose the snapshot of her father in a swimsuit on the dock. The picture was full of sunlight, and his smile was dazzling. That was the way she liked to think of him. Sybil slid her fingers under the snapshot, bending it only a little, and pulled it off the album page. "Don't lose it, though," Sybil said. "My mom never looks at these old albums, but with my luck she'll get a fit of nostalgia next week, and I'll get in a bunch of trouble."

"Hide the album," suggested Ari. "You'd better act like you can't find it, because chances are she'll dig it out tonight. Since she's run into me, I'm sure she'll be reminded of my dad."

Sybil grinned. "Good idea. You've got a natural aptitude for crime."

"I better go," said Ari. "I've got to show this to Paul."

Sybil walked Ari to the front door and waved to her. "If you see any more ghosts, let me know!" she called.

Ari hurried away down the block, averting her eyes from the haunted house. The last thing she wanted was to be known as the girl who was psychic. She wished she hadn't mentioned the ghost at all.

CHAPTER
FIFTEEN

PAUL STARED AT THE SNAPSHOT. "HE LOOKS SORT OF like me, all right."

"Sort of," said Ari. "But you look better."

"I don't know about that. He looks like the kind girls would go for."

"Sybil's mother seemed to go for him," said Ari. "She had lots and lots of pictures of him. They must have gone together for years. I wonder why they split up. You should have seen Mrs. Barron when she realized he was my dad. Anybody would have thought she'd spotted a rattlesnake."

"Maybe he cheated on her," said Paul.

The glare reflected off the water lit up her father's face and spotlighted his dazzling smile. He looked as if nothing bad could ever happen to him.

"He doesn't look like a drunk, does he?" said Paul. "He looks healthy."

"Maybe he wasn't a drunk back then," said Ari.

"I've got to get this picture back to Sybil. I only borrowed it."

"Let's take it somewhere and get it copied," suggested Paul. "I think there are camera shops that can do that. Are you pretty sure he was the one you saw at the dance, Ari?"

"I'm not sure of anything anymore," she admitted. "But it could have been. I was pretty shaken up and the light wasn't good. Besides, that snapshot must have been taken when he was about our age. By now he would have changed. It could have been him, though. And if it was, you have to admit that would explain the flour spill downstairs."

Paul chewed thoughtfully on his thumbnail. "Yeah, I guess he'd naturally come here to Aunt Gabrielle's to clean up."

"But if he's coming here to the house, why is he being so hush-hush about it?" cried Ari. "If he wants to see us, why doesn't he just come visit? What's the big deal?"

"Maybe it was him hiding behind that black mirror. Maybe he's looking us over to see if we're worth claiming," suggested Paul, with a trace of bitterness.

"All these years and not a word," said Ari. "Not even when Mamma died. The rat!" She thought of the vampire at the Boo Ball—his peremptory, overbearing manner. If that had been her father, no wonder she had hated him on sight. She clenched her fists. "I wish I'd been the one who dumped the flour on him."

"Don't you want to see him, though?" asked Paul. "In spite of all that?"

"I couldn't care less," said Ari coldly.

"Well, I'd like at least to get a look at him."

"After the way he's behaved?" cried Ari.

"I don't care," said Paul stubbornly. "At least I'd like to meet him."

"He's horrible," said Ari in a low voice.

"He's our father," said Paul. "I want to see him. I might ask Aunt Gabrielle if he's in town."

"You think she'd tell you?" asked Ari.

Paul made a face. "I don't know." He took the picture from Ari. "Anyway, we'll get the picture copied, one copy for each of us."

"Do whatever you want to with yours." Ari's eyes narrowed. "But I'm going to throw darts at mine."

Wednesday afternoon was foggy. Paul had begun training with the cross-country team and was slogging around the track with the others. He could hear ducks quacking somewhere in the mist. Probably they'd lost their way in the rain and had mistaken the school's playing fields for Rock Creek Park. He had lost sight of Sandy and was concentrating on his breathing. He was out of shape; that was for sure. He looked down at his white sweatshirt. "St. Anselm's Cross Country," it said, but he didn't feel like part of the team.

He was jogging around the track, going to class and doing his homework, but he felt as if he were holding his breath, expecting every minute that something overwhelming would happen.

Paul could hear his feet thudding against the

damp sand of the track. The back of his neck prickled as he heard a faint tuneless whistling. He stopped and listened, holding himself rigid. He could feel the cold fog settling on his bare skin and something else—a tight painful feeling in his chest.

Bryan ran by him. "You sprain an ankle or something, Montclair?" he panted.

Paul shook his head. He took a deep breath and set off running, but his concentration was shot. He had heard that whistling before, but the memory seemed just beyond his reach. He felt gooseflesh rise on his arms.

The lockers were in the activities building next to the gym. Sandy stepped out of the shower and toweled off, pink from head to toe. He pulled on his shorts. "You're going to run on Saturday, aren't you, Paul?"

Paul shrugged. "I guess." He tied his sneakers. "I'm out of shape, but it'll be good practice." He wondered if Sandy had heard that tuneless whistle out on the track. He didn't like to ask. He wasn't sure why. Maybe because it had given him the creeps.

"It's a long drive into town for me," said Sandy, rubbing his hair dry. "And the van leaves awfully early for the meet. It sure would be better if I could stay with somebody here in town the night before."

Paul barely heard him. He went on buttoning his shirt as if in a daze.

"Oh, come on, Paul. Can't you get a hint?" said

Sandy, exasperated. "Can I stay with you Friday night so I don't have to drive in for the meet Saturday morning?"

Paul laughed suddenly. He realized that Sandy was trying to get close to Ari. That was okay. Paul had seen Cos and Ari sneaking kisses around school lately, and it made him sick. "Sure. Spend the night at our place," said Paul. "That'd be great."

He had never checked out the guest bedroom across from Aunt Gabrielle's room, but when he thought of the dark shadows and the looming shapes upstairs, he suddenly was certain it would be better for Sandy to stay in his room, not down the hall. "Better bring a sleeping bag," he added. "I'm not sure what the extra bed situation is, but I know you can stay in my room." He grinned. "Ari's room is right next door to mine."

Sandy flushed self-consciously.

That evening, Paul checked with Aunt Gabrielle to see if it was okay for Sandy to stay over. She seemed to love the idea. "I'll have Carmel fix a nice roast," she said. "I know runners need good red meat to build up their blood." The tip of her pink tongue skated delicately across her lip, and Paul involuntarily took a step back. What was it about Aunt Gabrielle? he wondered nervously. When her eyes narrowed, a cold wind seemed to brush the back of his neck. With her deathly white skin and her thick black hair, she looked like an Egyptian queen just stepping out of a mummy case.

Ari seemed unaware of the chill that had fallen over her twin. She leaned serenely against the door to the kitchen and took a bite out of an apple. "Aunt Gabrielle, do you have any family albums? You know, photographs and stuff?"

Aunt Gabrielle gave a low, musical laugh that gurgled in her throat. She had an odd sort of laugh, with her lips only slightly parted. "We never went in much for photographs in our family, I'm afraid," she said. "I may have a few school photos somewhere of me as a little girl in braces, but I have no idea at all where they are. It's probably just as well. I must have been a dreadful child."

"No pictures of our dad either?" asked Ari.

"I'll look around," promised Aunt Gabrielle. "Surely I must have something of Richard. No, on second thought, he may have taken those with him."

Ari gave Paul a significant look. "Have you seen Dad lately?"

Aunt Gabrielle's hand went to her throat. "Why do you ask, dear?"

"Sybil had a picture of him in her family album," said Ari. "And I saw somebody who looked a lot like him at the Boo Ball. Whoever it was asked me to dance."

"Richard at a school dance?" Aunt Gabrielle was amused. "Oh, I don't think so. That wouldn't be his style at all."

"What is his style?" asked Paul.

"Life in the fast lane." Aunt Gabrielle made a vague, distracted gesture. "Richard never was attracted to the quiet life. He always went to extremes."

Ari thought of the serious-faced boy in the string quartet and wondered what had happened to change him into the man Aunt Gabrielle was describing. Had he suddenly hatched a new personality when he grew up? And could that happen to her and Paul, too? The idea made her uncomfortable.

After the twins went upstairs, they sat on Ari's bed talking. "Doesn't Aunt Gabrielle give you the creeps?" Paul asked.

"Sure," said Ari, surprised. "She's given me the creeps since the first night we met her."

Paul shivered. "Yeah, but just now—"

"What?" asked Ari eagerly. "What are you getting at?"

"I don't know," said Paul. "I just wish we knew what the heck was going on."

Ari stiffened suddenly. "Paul, maybe it's not a good idea for Sandy to spend the night here."

"It'll be fine," he said weakly. His imagination had gone into overdrive. Obviously Aunt Gabrielle was not some evil sorceress risen from the dead. What was he so wrought up about? "Probably Aunt Gabrielle figures Dad is a bad influence," Paul said, "so she's trying to keep him away from us." He desperately wanted to believe that nothing was wrong. "You know what a nut Aunt Gabrielle is about self-control," he said. "Maybe our dad makes a fool of himself at parties, drinks too much, wears lampshades on his head, or something like that."

"I saw him, Paul. You didn't." Ari shivered. "He scared me."

"You *think* you saw him." Paul paused a second, uncomfortably. "It was confusing that night. Everybody was in costume, and with that strobe light, half the people there looked like mass murderers."

"I don't care. I wish you'd tell Sandy he can't spend the night here."

Paul hesitated. Maybe Ari was right. But what explanation would he give to Sandy? "He's going to sleep right in my room," said Paul, frowning. "What can go wrong?"

CHAPTER
SIXTEEN

CARMEL OUTDID HERSELF WITH THE FEAST SHE SERVED the night Sandy came. The chandelier shimmered overhead and a splendid brown roast with little potatoes, onions, and carrots sat at the center of the gleaming mahogany table. Dinner had been served late, and it had a special, formal feeling.

"Does your aunt always serve wine with the meals?" Sandy whispered to Paul.

"Pretty much," he answered. But often he had noticed after dinner that her glass was untouched. She served wine, but she never seemed to drink it. Tonight, however, Paul had seen her lift the glass to her lips. Her cheeks were pink and her violet eyes shone.

After Sandy poured himself another glass, Paul moved the wine bottle out of reach. He didn't want Sandy to get drunk. He was beginning to wonder if he had had too much himself. The wine in Aunt Gabrielle's glass looked funny to him somehow, thicker than the wine in his own glass. It seemed to cling to the sides of the glass as if it were sticky. When she put it down, it sloshed slightly, a deep ruby-red. Paul glanced up at his aunt and was startled to see that her violet eyes were jewel-like, glowing as if they were lit from within. Paul gasped. "I think I need some fresh air," he said. He hastily pushed his chair away from the table and lurched toward the large French doors. He stumbled outside into the chill night air of the terrace. He could feel the uneven bricks under his feet, and nearby a tree creaked as it moved in the breeze. As he gulped in air, his eyes fell to the flower beds that edged the brick pavement. In the dim light, he made out a bit of brown—a small piece of fur, its hair shining in the light cast by the big windows. *That shouldn't be there,* he thought. He remembered how the man at Aunt Gabrielle's party had passed out standing in this precise spot, his fat body crumpling like a folding paper fan. Paul's head spun with formless images, swirling shapes, pinwheels, and black spots, and he felt himself sway.

Ari's voice suddenly brought him to his senses with a start. "Paul," Ari cried. "Are you all right?" He felt her grab his arm.

Wordlessly, Paul gestured toward the pathetic pelt of fur.

Ari stooped to look at it, then hastily straightened up. Her face was pale in the uncertain light. "It's all right," she said. "It's only a dead rat. It's just that something has—has bitten off its head." The twins stared at each other for a long moment. Ari's eyes were wide and luminous in the dim light. Her dark hair fell in glossy waves to her shoulders. In the dim light, she looked frighteningly like Aunt Gabrielle and Paul gulped. "A cat must have got it," she went on breathlessly. "That's what's happened."

"Sure," said Paul. He supposed he should push the rat's oddly flattened body under one of the azaleas so Carmel wouldn't get an unpleasant shock when she saw it, but he couldn't bring himself to touch it. Ari seemed in no rush to move it, either. "I think I'd better lay off the wine from now on," said Paul. He glanced at the big lighted windows of the dining room. Aunt Gabrielle's back was to them, and she appeared in silhouette, a dark figure with a faint glimmer of jeweled combs in her upswept hair. Across from her, Sandy, his face flushed, drained his wineglass.

"You'd better go in and get the bottle away from Sandy," said Ari. "If we're not careful, he's going to be sliding under the table in a minute."

The twins opened the French doors. Aunt Gabrielle regarded them anxiously as they came in. "Are you all right, Paul? I hope dinner wasn't too rich. Carmel has a heavy hand with the butter."

"Dinner was fine—delicious, in fact," said Paul. He had to grab on to the back of a chair to steady himself. He made his way around the table to his place and took the bottle of wine from Sandy's hands. "I think Sandy and me had better lay off the wine, Aunt Gabrielle," said Paul. "We've got a race tomorrow."

"Of course." Aunt Gabrielle smiled. "It was thoughtless of me to put it out." She pressed the cork back in the bottle and it slid in with a protesting squeak. She placed it on the sideboard next to the brandy decanter.

Paul caught himself staring at his aunt. Her slender figure was encased in a clinging cashmere dress of lavender. The skirt fell in soft folds to the floor and moved gently as she turned to face them with a smile. Her arms were bare—the dress had only thin little straps—and Paul could make out the delicate bones in her chest, her skin stretched tightly over them. Paul thought the room was a bit chilly, but Aunt Gabrielle was wearing far fewer clothes than either he or Ari, and she showed no signs of gooseflesh. A chill shook him. "We have to get up early," said Paul suddenly. "Maybe we'd better turn in now."

"It is late," agreed Ari, rising hastily.

"Nice dinner," said Sandy. "Real nice."

"I'm glad you enjoyed it." Aunt Gabrielle smiled her strange half-smile.

Together the twins helped Sandy down the long hallway. His steps were uncertain as they mounted the stairs, and the twins were half-supporting him. "Ari," said Sandy, "do you know that song 'AchyBreaky Heart'?"

"I've heard it once or twice," said Ari cautiously.

"It makes me think of you," said Sandy. "All the

songs I hear make me think of you."

Paul wondered exactly how much Sandy had had to drink. He wasn't going to be much good to the team nursing a hangover.

"Do boys ever tell you you're beautiful?" Sandy went on.

Ari dimpled. "Constantly."

"I was afraid of that," said Sandy.

Ari watched anxiously as Paul guided his friend into his bedroom. "Better lock the connecting door," Paul told his twin in a low voice.

Paul hadn't drunk as much as Sandy, but he felt sick. He helped Sandy get in his pajamas and unrolled the sleeping bag. Sandy snuggled into it at once and made a comical snuffling sound. Paul went into his bathroom and got an aspirin for his aching head. When he got back, Sandy was snoring softly. Paul put on his pajamas, then pushed aside the curtains and stared at the terrace below. In the light cast on the terrace, he saw a slender shadow moving back and forth. Aunt Gabrielle was clearing the table, he realized. Paul felt a flash of anger. What had she meant by serving Sandy all that wine? She knew they were competing first thing in the morning.

He let the curtain drop from his hands, slid into bed, and pulled the covers up to his chin. He slept fitfully. The moonlight and the sighing night wind disturbed him. Tossing, half-awake, he felt his flesh prickle with unease.

Suddenly his eyes were drawn to Sandy's sleeping bag. A woman in a cloak had bent over him.

Paul noticed that her cloak moved and shifted easily, as if it were made of something lighter and more fluid than cloth—mist perhaps. Its folds billowed and shifted around her as she looked up. Paul was shocked to see that her face was the face of the skull hidden in the mantelpiece—the jaw hung loosely, held only with flabby shreds of rotting flesh. Bat's teeth grinned at him, and in the eye sockets, lavender eyes glowed with an eerie iridescence. It was Aunt Gabrielle! She was dead!

He sat bolt upright.

Aunt Gabrielle was kneeling beside Sandy's sleeping bag. Her dress was gray in the dark.

"Aunt Gabrielle!" Paul cried.

She lifted her head slowly, her jeweled combs glinting. Then she turned and smiled at him. To his relief, her face showed the faint pink of life. She was not a skeleton at all; he had only been dreaming. He hugged himself and shivered.

"I thought I'd better check on the dear boy," she said softly. "I'm afraid I shouldn't have let him have that wine, Paul. I blame myself." She raised a finger to her lips. "Shh—let's be careful not to wake him up." She rose and glided toward the door, passing by the foot of Paul's bed where a band of light from the window fell on her flushed face. She seemed especially lovely, and she moved with an uncanny smoothness, like a sleepwalker. "Sleep tight," she whispered. The door closed behind her.

Paul wasn't sure how long he sat in bed, staring at Sandy's still form in the sleeping bag. He could make out the spiky outline of Sandy's hair, but he was afraid to go over and look in his friend's face. He was afraid of what he might see. He leapt out of bed and rapped on the door.

It opened at once, as if Ari had been waiting for his signal. She stood before him in her flowing white nightgown, her eyes wide with fear. The windowpanes showed the first trace of the pale light that comes before dawn. "Ari," Paul gasped. "Aunt Gabrielle came in my room just now!"

Ari stared at him, white-faced with shock.

"She was bending over Sandy," said Paul hoarsely.

"Is he all right?" cried Ari.

The twins rushed back into Paul's room and Ari bent over Sandy in unconscious imitation of Aunt Gabrielle's motion. Paul could hardly bear to look.

"He's breathing," Ari said, with a frightened glance over her shoulder. "I think he's okay."

Paul sat down suddenly on his bed and wiped his palm over his damp brow. "I thought—jeez, to tell you the truth, I don't know what I thought. All kinds of crazy things! I must have been going out of my mind." He shuddered. "I was having a nightmare. When I woke up, I was actually afraid to look at him."

The alarm buzzed and Sandy stirred. Ari stood up quickly. She flashed Paul a smile as she reached for the door. "Good luck with the race!" she whispered. She slipped back into her room.

Sandy's eyes flew open. "What time is it?" he said thickly.

Paul glanced at the clock. "Five o'clock. Time to hit the road."

Sandy groaned. "I feel terrible."

Paul's heart raced, but after a second he said, "You shouldn't have drunk all that wine, man."

"I know," said Sandy, clutching a hand to his head. "Never again. Don't tell Coach, okay?"

"No problem," agreed Paul. There was a lot he didn't want to tell Coach. He only wished he had followed Ari's advice and not let Sandy sleep over.

As the team van sped along the highway, Sandy seemed dazed. He looked out the window at nothing in particular. Farm fenceposts cast long shadows on the grass that verged the highway. They were far from the city.

A teammate nudged Paul. "Look at Sandy," he said. "He's out of it. He must be in love." A couple of other guys laughed, but when Paul glanced at Sandy's glassy eyes, the laughter died in his throat.

At last they saw the fluttering flags and the large sign that announced they had arrived at the meet. A clutch of vans were already parked on the bare clay at the edge of the course.

"We're running kind of late," said the coach, frowning. "But most of you know this course. Paul, you'd better walk over it and familiarize yourself with it. It's pretty well-marked."

Paul set out alone to walk the course. The flags marking the route fluttered in the cold breeze. Leaden clouds obscured the sky, and Paul felt oppressed by the gloomy day. The race didn't seem to matter to him anymore. He turned around abruptly and walked back. He could see the bright colors of the team vans directly ahead. Coach had gathered the team into a group for a last-minute pep talk. Sandy's back was to Paul, but he was easy to recognize with his bristled reddish hair. Suddenly Sandy's head dipped and he fell forward. Two boys grabbed him and laid him on his back. Paul ran over to the group in horror.

"He's fainted," said Coach. His fingers were on Sandy's wrist, checking his pulse.

Sandy stirred. "Wha—?" he said, struggling to get up.

"You stay right there, Sandy," said Coach.

Mr. Tomlin, the assistant coach, knelt beside Sandy on the other side. "How do you feel, son?"

"Okay." Sandy tried to prop himself up on his elbows.

"No need to rush to get up," said Coach. His steady gaze met Coach Tomlin's. "We're going to have to take him in to the hospital to be checked out. You'd better go with me, Tommy. One of us has to keep an eye on the boy and one of us has to drive."

"I'll go with you," said Paul suddenly.

"You aren't going to run today?" asked Coach Tomlin.

Paul shook his head. "I couldn't," he said.

A glance at Paul's face must have convinced the coach he was in no shape to run. It was soon settled that Paul and Coach would take Sandy to the emergency room. They helped him to the van.

"I'm okay," Sandy protested. "You don't have to help me. I can walk."

"No sense taking any chances," said Coach. "You keep your arms around our necks. Have you been feeling sick, son?"

Sandy shot Paul an anguished glance. Paul knew he was worried that the coach would find out about all the wine he had drunk. "I'm okay," Sandy mumbled. "Honest."

"He seemed kind of out of it on the trip over," Paul volunteered. "And he looks awfully pale, doesn't he?"

Paul could tell by the set expression of the coach's lips that he was worried. Once they got out on the highway, Paul watched the needle of the speedometer creep steadily upward.

At last they arrived at a hospital entrance marked "EMERGENCY." Paul and Coach supported Sandy as he got out of the van. Awkwardly the three of them made their way to the lighted doors. As the automatic glass doors swung open before them, Sandy suddenly sagged against Paul. "He's fainted again," cried Paul, catching him under the other arm. A wheelchair materialized almost at once, and a moment later Sandy was whisked into the examining room. Paul had visited the emergency room once or twice and he knew that people could sit for hours there waiting their turn, but evidently being unconscious qualified Sandy to move to the front of the line. Coach and Paul went into the examining room with him. Sandy winced as a nurse pricked his finger.

"Hemoglobin count very low," a white-coated doctor said moments later, pulling on fleshy latex gloves. "The kid hardly has any blood left in him. We're going to have to do a transfusion. Can you give us permission?"

"Yes," Coach said steadily, but he was as white as chalk. "I need a phone. I've got to call the boy's parents."

The doctor glanced at Paul. "You better sit down," he said. "We don't need to have another one passing out on us."

Paul sank into a plastic chair next to the examining table. Sandy was on a stretcher now, not moving.

"Is he going to be all right?" Paul asked faintly.

"Don't worry," said the doctor. "He's in good hands. We've just got to get some blood into him."

White-coated orderlies wheeled Sandy out of the examining room. Coach talked to the doctor privately a moment over in a corner. Paul watched Coach dial Sandy's parents on the pay phone in the waiting room. It seemed he was on the phone a long time. When he returned, he placed a hand on Paul's shoulder. "No sense in you hanging around, Paul. They're going to keep Sandy overnight. Can you get somebody to come get you? I'm going to have to wait here for his folks."

"I'll have my sister come get me," said Paul. "You do think he's going to be all right, don't you, Coach?"

"You heard the doctor. He's in good hands," said Coach, but his eyes looked strained. "He's bleeding internally somehow, and it'll take them a while to figure out where. The doctor said that with as much blood as he had lost, he shouldn't have been able to stand up. Probably he wouldn't have been able to get out of bed this morning if he hadn't been a runner. Runners' blood carries so much oxygen that they can get by on less of it than most folks." Coach wiped his brow with a handkerchief. "Modern medicine is amazing. Don't you worry. They'll fix him up."

Ari got to the hospital even before Sandy's parents did.

"How fast did you drive, Ari?" asked Paul irritably. He grabbed her arm and they hurried out to the parking lot. He scowled, wanting deep inside to throw his arms around her and weep.

"I was worried!" Ari said. "Sure, I was speeding. I couldn't make any sense out of what you were saying, Paul. What's wrong with Sandy?"

"Let's get out of this place." Paul pulled the car door open. "Coach has been asking me if Sandy was acting funny, and the last thing I want is for Sandy's parents to start asking me the same thing."

"He did drink a lot last night," said Ari.

Paul shot her a scornful look as they sped out of the parking lot. "Overdoing it on wine usually doesn't put guys in the hospital," he said.

"Well, what's wrong with him, then?"

They drove for a moment in silence. "Ari, the doctor said he hardly had any blood left in him."

Ari stared blankly at the road ahead. "But what can that mean?"

"It means Aunt Gabrielle was sucking the

blood out of him last night!" cried Paul. "That's what it means. He was white as a sheet on the drive out here, completely out of it. That's why she came in my room last night—she wanted Sandy's blood."

Ari laid a hand on Paul's arm. "You're upset. You're not thinking straight."

Paul shook off her hand impatiently. "Cut it out, Ari. Sure, I'm freaking out. I've got a good reason to freak out. You know that dead rat we saw on the terrace last night?"

Ari nodded. Her eyes were frightened.

"Aunt Gabrielle bit off its head. I bet you rat's blood was in her wineglass last night. That's why it looked thicker than wine. Didn't you notice the way it sort of stuck to the sides of the glass? It was already coagulating. Usually she doesn't touch her wine, but she drank it all last night, all right." Paul laughed shortly. "She didn't like the taste of it much. I remember she sort of screwed up her face when she drank it. She probably liked Sandy's blood better. Good, oxygen-rich runner's blood." Paul shot Ari a bitter look. "Once I get back into shape, maybe I'll be the next one on the dinner list."

Large signs over the highway indicated that the junction with Route 295 was coming up soon. "We can't go back to the house now," Ari said suddenly. "Go downtown. We need to find a place we can talk."

Paul changed lanes as if in a dream. The sky overhead was dark, draining the scene of all color.

A thunderstorm would almost be a relief, he thought. Tension lay heavy in the air, and his skin felt tight. Out of the corner of his eye, he saw Ari's shirt rising and falling with her quick breath. If she hadn't been there, he would have gone crazy.

A half hour later, Paul pulled the car into a vacant parking spot in front of the National Gallery. He and Ari thrust their hands in their pockets, bent against the cold breeze, and silently mounted the tall steps. An elevator took them down to the lower level. Paul heard the soothing spattering of the artificial waterfall and headed in that direction, following the signs to the cafeteria.

Luckily, the tables were mostly empty. Only a few arty-looking people dressed in black and wearing handcrafted jewelry sipped tea and ate croissants by some potted palms. The twins found a table and turned their chairs to face the falling water. Paul hoped its white noise would help keep anyone from overhearing what he had to say.

"It all adds up," he told Ari grimly. "Aunt Gabrielle never goes out in the sun—and I mean never. We should have realized what that meant. Haven't you seen those old vampire movies when Dracula hears the rooster crow and gets real nervous? Next thing you know, he's running back to his coffin to hide before the sun comes up. Sun must be poison for vampires. When you think about it, that must be why Aunt Gabrielle couldn't come to Mom's funeral. It wasn't that she had the flu. She simply didn't dare go out in the sun."

"She took us to St. Anselm's that first day," argued Ari, "when she registered us for classes."

"It was raining," said Paul. "Remember? Not a chance of any sun. And she wore that big floppy hat even then."

"I think she's always trying to protect her complexion," said Ari.

Paul snorted. "Remember that poor guy we thought she was making out with after the dinner party? He had to be helped to his car."

"Shh!" Ari whispered. She glanced around nervously. "Don't shout."

"What other woman goes jogging around Georgetown alone after dark?" asked Paul. "Aunt Gabrielle's not jogging, Ari! She's going hunting!"

"What are you saying, Paul?" Ari's voice trembled.

"You want me to spell it out for you? Aunt Gabrielle is a vampire!"

Ari cast a glance at some people sitting a few tables away. A few words floated over the sound of the waterfall. "—tonal values—Matisse-like, don't you think?"

Ari leaned close to Paul. "But there's no such thing as vampires," she whispered harshly.

"Tell that to Aunt Gabri," said Paul. "Better yet, tell it to poor Sandy. They're pumping blood into him right this minute."

"There's got to be some kind of logical explanation," insisted Ari.

"Maybe." Paul grabbed Ari's hand and looked

her in the eyes. "But you know in your heart that this is the right one."

The twins looked at each other for a long minute.

"Ari," Paul whispered finally, "what if our dad's a vampire, too?"

Ari ran her fingers through her hair frantically. "What are we going to do?"

CHAPTER
SEVENTEEN

THE TWINS WERE SILENT AS THEY DROVE TOWARD THE town house. They gazed out the car windows. The ordinary life of the city was going on as if nothing had changed. A delivery van pulled abreast of them at a traffic light. THE LAME DUCK RESTAURANT, the lettering on its side proclaimed. LET US WOK AND ROLL YOU. A woman carrying a shiny plastic dry-cleaning bag passed by. Standing at the corner, waiting for the light, was an old man in a Stetson hat. Silver rosettes ringed the crown of his hat. Then the light changed and the traffic surged ahead. The twins moved on, oblivious to the normal world around them.

"We could search Aunt Gabrielle's room while she's out jogging," Paul said suddenly.

"Paul!" Ari was aghast.

"I hear that during the daytime vampires sleep in their coffins," Paul insisted. "If we found a coffin in her bedroom that would prove it."

"We can't search Aunt Gabrielle's room," said Ari. "She's been so nice to us! That would be an awful thing to do."

"She's probably hidden the coffin anyway," said Paul gloomily.

Ari eyed him uneasily. "Maybe we ought to call the hospital and check on how Sandy is getting on before we do anything we might regret."

"You keep thinking there's going to be some reasonable explanation for all this, don't you? We're going to call the hospital, and it'll turn out Sandy's got a bleeding ulcer, and Aunt Gabrielle is a nice lady with a sun allergy, and everything's just fine and dandy."

"No," Ari said slowly. "I guess I don't really think that." She had thought from the first that Aunt Gabrielle was strange. Nothing in the past weeks had altered that first impression.

"Remember last night in the dining room?" Paul said. "She was wearing that thin dress with the itty-bitty straps, and she wasn't a bit cold. No sign of goose bumps. She's not human, Ari!"

Ari was surprised that she didn't feel more shocked at what Paul was saying. She supposed she had suspected something was amiss all along. After all, she had noticed right off that Aunt Gabri wasn't in any way like an ordinary middle-aged woman. No bags sagged under her eyes, no crow's-feet appeared at the corners of her eyes when she smiled, and she had none of the usual comfortable padding of fat that middle-aged people have. Her lips were cold. Her eyes were that unearthly lavender. Small things, maybe, but they added up. Ari gazed out the window. Ahead she could see the gilt weather vane on top of the clock of the Crestan Bank Building. They were almost home.

When the twins drove up to the house, they were startled to see that the curtains of the living room were closed. They stared at each other a moment, not sure what to think. Paul pulled the Mazda into the garage and they got out. A cold wind drove rattling leaves down the walk as they mounted the front steps. A vase stood outside the black-lacquered front door, its mixed flowers nodding in the breeze, an incongruous splash of color. Ari slid her key into the lock, and the twins held their breath as they stepped into the house.

The big doors to the living room had been drawn back, and Aunt Gabrielle lay stretched out on the striped satin sofa. Her brow creased, her hand held to her temple, she looked as if she had a bad headache. She wore black satin pajamas and cutaway slippers that revealed bony, high-arched feet. "My darlings," she cried, sitting up suddenly. She patted a spot beside her on the sofa. "Come sit beside me. We must talk, my pets."

Paul had a sudden urge to pull the twisted satin cord and open the heavy velvet curtains to the sunlight; then he remembered that the day was so gloomy that would prove nothing. It was dim in the living room now, but it would scarcely be less dim if he pulled the curtains back.

He took a seat on one of the chairs opposite

the couch. He noticed that Ari did the same. Clearly neither of them wanted to sit next to Aunt Gabrielle. Neither even wanted to be in her reach. Paul stared at his aunt, hoping that his suspicions would seem ridiculous once he looked at her. But the more closely he looked, the more she seemed to him like a vampire. Her skin was unearthly white. It wasn't like ordinary skin at all. And her violet eyes seemed to glow as if lit from within.

Aunt Gabrielle pressed a bony hand to her head and sighed. "I loathe emotional scenes," she said. "As you know, moderation in all things is my motto. I have never cared for living from crisis to crisis the way your father does."

Paul glanced at Ari. He was in no mood to hear another lecture on the virtues of self-control. He began to speak, but Aunt Gabrielle raised a hand. "No, hear me out, dear." She took a deep shuddering breath. "I am going to have a little party this evening," she said. "A small soiree to introduce you to some intimate family friends. I want you both to be sure to be there, so don't make any other plans."

"I wish you would answer a few questions for us first," said Ari. A glint of determination shone in her eyes.

Aunt Gabrielle made a gesture with one bony hand as if she were pushing Ari away. "Not now, my dear ones, not now. I need my beauty sleep. After the party tonight, we'll talk. But please don't go all priggish and judgmental on me, my dear. I couldn't endure it if you turned into some insufferable puritan. I'm sure I don't need to say another word about that. You are such a sweet, sensitive child." She rose from the couch, and with a sad smile, she glided through the open door. A moment later, they heard the clack of the heels of her slippers on the stairs.

Paul stood up. "'Moderation in all things,'" he mocked her mincing voice. "She didn't use much moderation when she went after Sandy, did she?"

Ari cast an anxious glance at the staircase across the hall. "Hush, Paul, what if she hears you?"

"It doesn't matter if she does. She must know we're onto her. Otherwise what's that stuff about how she hates big emotional scenes? I don't see any point in waiting until after her stupid party."

Ari realized that she herself shrank from big emotional scenes. When it had come right down to it, she hadn't been able to press Aunt Gabrielle for answers. But Paul was right. They couldn't go on like this. She forced herself to unclench her fists and breathe deeply.

"I don't know," Paul continued, clutching a hand to his belly. "I feel like something's jumping around in my stomach. Maybe we shouldn't talk to her at all. Maybe we ought to clear out and run like hell."

Ari nodded. She had the sensation that the shadows in the hallway stirred with life. The wind that swept past the lacquered black door outside sighed and moaned in an unearthly voice. Even the electric sconces on the walls seemed to move a bit in her peripheral vision, as if the lights were held by unseen hands.

The twins tiptoed upstairs. They cast a fearful glance at the closed door of their aunt's bedroom as they passed it. Ari thought of the fanged man with the aquiline nose who had visited her room early one morning, casting his crooked shadow on her wall. He had looked like her father, she thought. But his hand had not warmed the door-knob. Had it been her father? Or a ghost or shadow of her father, similar to the ghost she had seen on Dunbarton Street of the party guest who had never left?

In Paul's room, the twins sat facing each other on the bed. "This is so awful," said Ari. "We can't tell anybody. I can't breathe a word to Cos or even to Sybil. They'd think I was certifiable if I told them what was going on."

"I'm not so sure of that," said Paul. "We can't be the only ones who've noticed that there's some-thing weird about Aunt Gabrielle."

The twins emptied their wallets, spreading a few crumpled bills and change out on the bed-spread. "That's it," said Paul. "Barely twenty dol-lars. But I've still got six hundred in the bank left over from my summer job. What about you?"

Ari sighed. "Three hundred, maybe. Baby-sit-ting doesn't pay very well."

"We could get back to New Orleans on what we've got," Paul said. "But I don't know what we'd live on once we got there, and the problem is Aunt Gabrielle would know right where to look for us. All she'd have to do is ask around and she'd find us in a matter of hours."

Ari blinked rapidly. "What if she sent the police after us?"

"I don't think she'd call the police," said Paul. "She's got too much to hide." He stuffed the bills back into his wallet. "I wish I knew more about vampires. We've got to figure out some way to protect ourselves, Ari. What about that garlic and crucifix stuff? I wonder if that would work."

Ari shook her head. "Carmel practically bathes in garlic. Think of her spaghetti sauce."

Paul nodded. "I've seen a gold cross around Carmel's neck, too, and that's never bothered Aunt Gabrielle. The garlic and crucifix stuff must not work."

"What about a stake in the heart?" suggested Ari.

Paul stared at her. "Good grief, Ari. I couldn't drive a stake into Aunt Gabrielle's heart! What do you think I am?"

Ari knew she couldn't drive a stake in her aunt's heart, either. She shrugged ruefully.

"One thing we *do* know is that Aunt Gabrielle can't take the sun," said Paul. "She never goes out in it. So that's something we can bank on."

"I've noticed something else," said Ari. "She never has a fire in the fireplace, not even on cold, gloomy days like this, not even gas logs. And she never lights any candles for dinner. All the candlesticks in the dining room are wired for electric bulbs."

"Tacky," commented Paul.

"That's why it's significant," said Ari. "Aunt

Gabrielle usually has wonderful taste. My guess is that vampires can't stand fire."

"Now we're getting somewhere." Paul's eyes narrowed. "Yeah, think about it. The kitchen is all-electric. She's got a microwave and the electric range. Yeah, I think you're onto something."

"But Paul . . ." Ari hesitated, "we don't really want to hurt Aunt Gabrielle, do we?"

"That depends," said Paul. "I sure as heck don't want to end up like Sandy. We have to be ready to defend ourselves. We need to be able to make her back off if things get out of hand."

"I think I've got an idea," said Ari suddenly.

The twins went together to M Street, the main shopping street of the district. When they returned, they had cigarette lighters tucked in their pockets.

The caterer was pushing open the front door when they got back to the house. His arms were full of flowers. "Ciao, kids," he trilled. "I adore your aunt's parties. No penny-pinching—everything strictly first class. Lots of times they tell me, 'Do it cheap but make it look expensive.' But no problems like that with your aunt. She pays extra for a rush job like this without a peep. And she's one who understands quality." The young man hurried down the checkerboard hallway and through the open door of the dining room. Ari saw him fussing with the flowers on the buffet table.

"I wonder what's with this party of hers," Paul said. "She came up with the idea all of a sudden.

You heard the guy—'a rush job', he said." Paul paused at the foot of the stairs. "What's she up to? I wish I knew."

"Whatever it is," said Ari, "we're ready. If we get in a tight place—"

"We'll use these," Paul interrupted, pulling his lighter out of his pocket and twirling the flint. The lighter's thin blue-and-yellow flame was a tiny spot of brightness in the shadows. Ari was suddenly terrified. How much protection could a small flame really be against a vampire? It was all they had.

CHAPTER
EIGHTEEN

ARI AND PAUL STOOD TOGETHER BESIDE THE DINNER gong at the back of the hall, watching the slender, chic party guests greet one another with shrill cries of joy. It was dark outside, but inside crystal, jewels, and shimmering satin gleamed in the lamplight.

After some anxious discussion, the twins had decided it was best to stand near the three exits at the back of the house in case anything terrible happened. Paul imagined himself giving the dinner gong a kick to create a diversion, then grabbing Ari and diving over the spread of fruit and cold cuts on the dining room table and bursting out the French doors. He had seen that sort of maneuver lots of times in movies. He was a little uncertain how it would work out in actual practice.

But as the living room and dining room filled up with guests, Paul felt the muscles at the back of his neck unclenching. He recognized a few of the guests from Aunt Gabrielle's last party—the graphic designer, Gwendolyn, for instance. Tonight she was wearing a gauzy dress in a beige flower print. Peeking out from the folds of the skirt were the toes of what looked like combat boots. The retired ballet dancer, Tippi, arrived a few minutes later with Derek, the cave-cheeked rock singer. Tonight he was wearing tight black pants and a white satin shirt unbuttoned to the navel. The familiar faces were reassuring enough to Paul that he decided to visit the buffet table. He filled a plate with frosted grapes, a wedge of Brie cheese, and some dry crackers.

Then he spotted a beautiful blonde about his age. Her straight blond hair fell in a silken fringe to her shoulders, and the black velvet scoop-necked top she wore revealed startling cleavage. Paul poured himself a glass of champagne and smiled. "Hullo," he said. "Are you a friend of my aunt?"

"Sort of," she said. "Friend of a friend, anyway." Her voice was high and flutelike.

"The reason I ask is she said something about having a soiree for her most intimate friends," said Paul. "Just an expression, I guess."

The girl smiled. "Nobody's got a hundred intimate friends, you know. Probably she tried to invite some people who were close to your age so you wouldn't be bored."

"That must be it. Can I get you something to drink?" asked Paul.

"No, thank you," she said. "By the way, I'm Verena."

"I guess you know my name," he said.

"Oh, yes." She smiled sweetly. "You're Paul."

"Where are you in school, Verena?" he asked.

"I'm not exactly in school right now," she said. "But I used to go to St. Anne's."

Paul frowned. Ari had mentioned St. Anne's School for Girls. Wasn't that where Sybil's mom went back in the old days? It had been next door to St. Anselm's, but St. Anselm's absorbed it when it went coed. "How long ago was that?" he asked.

"Oh, a while," she said. Her lovely chin had a slight cleft and a dimple teased the corner of her mouth. "School was interfering with other things I really wanted to do. It seemed like a waste of time, and it started so early in the morning!"

Paul met her eyes. "I guess you like to sleep all day."

The girl's shapely hand splayed over her mouth as she giggled. "I guess I do," she admitted. "I watch a lot of late-night TV. It probably rots my brain."

Paul looked her up and down. "It hasn't hurt your figure, anyway."

She laughed suddenly, and Paul saw the flash of her fangs. Her skin, though pale, was translucent and flawless. Tiny diamond earrings glittered in each pale earlobe, and her dress, slit up to the thigh, revealed the sort of legs featured in stocking ads.

"How long have you been a vampire?" asked Paul, trying to affect a conversational tone.

Verena looked embarrassed. "Thirty-five years. You don't think I'm too old for you, do you? You know, once vampires get made, they don't get any older, really."

Paul felt queasy. "Made?" he asked in a faint voice.

Verena leaned so close to him that he backed away. "It's great," she breathed. "Better than sex."

"No bad side effects at all?" Paul glanced over his shoulder. He wished he could get away from the girl, but he felt as if he were held to her by strong rubber bands. The girl's magnetic green eyes grew bright, then dimmed as if they were battery powered. She laid a cool white hand on his neck, and he felt himself tingle from head to foot. He glanced down and was horrified to see her fingers had left a phosphorescent glow on his skin.

"It would be beautiful," she breathed. "I'd suck out your blood until you were too weak to move and you could feel my heart beating. Then I'd bite a vein, and let my blood mix with yours. Vampire blood is eternal. You'd feel wonderful, I promise you, and you'd never, never die. You'll be sixteen forever."

"But let me get this straight," said Paul nervously. "I'd already be dead, wouldn't I? I mean, my blood would be basically gone, wouldn't it?" He ran his hand over his neck where she had touched him, relieved to see the phosphorescence was fading.

She giggled. "Well, sure, if you want to get technical about it. But you'd have vampire blood instead, and that's so much better. It's so intense—so deep."

"Sure. You get to watch all those late-night TV shows," said Paul.

"No, stupid." Verena leaned very close to him. He could see the dark sweep of her eyelashes and the fine lines of color that radiated from her jewel-like irises, and he felt himself losing his grip. "I mean, you and me," Verena said softly, "drunk on each other's blood, our hearts beating as one. Let me do it, Paul. It would be perfect."

Verena's head suddenly jerked back, and Paul was astonished to see his aunt push herself between them. Her bony hand was firmly on Verena's beautiful chest. She pushed the younger woman away. "Give the boy some air, Verena," said Aunt Gabrielle briskly.

"I find Paul so very attractive," purred Verena.

Aunt Gabrielle dusted an imaginary crumb off Paul's shirt. "I'm sure you do." She smiled. "But let's try to behave ourselves, dear. You're in a civilized household tonight. Come with me, Paul. There are some people I'd like you to meet."

"Well, nice meeting you, Verena," Paul said as he backed away.

"I'm sorry about Verena," said Aunt Gabrielle in a low voice. "She's a lovely girl, but sometimes I do wonder about her self-control. Why don't you go find Ari? Something tells me you could use a breather from my friends."

Paul found Ari by the fireplace. She was pulling grapes one by one off a bunch with her teeth. Paul touched her shoulder and she jumped.

"I've been propositioned by a vampire," he said gloomily. "She wants to mingle my blood with hers. When she was talking to me, I couldn't think straight. I looked into her eyes and it started to sound good. I swear for half a second I was ready to take her up on it. I wonder if she put something in my drink."

"You're scaring me, Paul," Ari stuttered. "Are you making this up?"

"I wish." He took a gulp from his glass. "Maybe I'm past being scared." He glanced around. "When you think about it, they're all sort of like Aunt Gabrielle, aren't they? I almost feel at home. By the way, they aren't eating. Have you noticed? We're the only ones who've touched the food."

"Maybe they're on diets." Ari's eyes darted nervously around the room. "They're all very thin."

"They're all vampires, that's why. Check out the blonde over there in the low-cut velvet top."

"Very pretty," said Ari.

"That's the one that propositioned me. She's about fifty years old, I figure, and she's got fangs."

"She only looks about eighteen." Ari craned her neck to see.

"They don't get older once they become vampires. That's how Aunt Gabrielle avoids wrinkles. Check out the blonde again—see the fangs?"

"No," said Ari. "She keeps covering her mouth."

"She's hiding her fangs." Paul looked around the room. The place was so full of expensively dressed, handsome, skinny people that it looked like an ad in a glossy magazine. "Oh, what the hell." He refilled his glass from a bottle on the mantel and sipped it delicately. "Hey, what do you know? It's wine," he said.

Ari stared at him. "What did you expect?"

"You can't be too careful in a crowd like this. Could be blood," he said. "Betcha the others aren't drinking wine." He glanced around. "Since we're here, we might as well find out all we can." He downed his wine rapidly and smiled at Ari. "Well, here goes." He turned and waded out into the thickest part of the crowd.

A slender young man immediately filled Paul's place. He gazed down at Ari. "Did anyone ever tell you that you're beautiful?" he asked.

"Yes, and I'm tired of hearing it," she said firmly.

He looked hurt. "You don't have much small talk, do you?"

"I have a boyfriend," she said.

He took her hand and suddenly an electric shock froze her. A sharp pain ran through her from her head to her toes and her fingers spread out, splayed by the sudden shock. Her eyes flew open in horror. What was happening to her?

"I am sure we have so much in common," he whispered softly in her ear. Before Ari could protest, the vampire sat on her lap. She felt the cold wetness of his mouth on the flesh of her neck.

"No!" she cried, tossing her head suddenly. She

struggled to her feet, and to her relief the vampire slipped off her lap. She stumbled away from him, frightened by his angry glare.

A tough-looking man in a T-shirt leaned toward her. "You and Jep didn't hit it off, huh?" He smiled, showing fangs. A single gold earring gleamed in his nostril.

Ari backed away from him. She wouldn't let him touch her, she thought, her heart pounding. She would kick him. But did vampires feel pain? The mantel bit into her shoulder blades. She pictured the death's head skull in the fireplace inches away from her fingers, and her stomach heaved. "Get away from me," she said. "I hate you."

"That doesn't bother me." He laughed. "I kind of like it when girls squirm. I get off on disgust."

Ari felt herself go cold. With a sudden movement, she dipped to her knees and, taking advantage of his surprise, scooted around the couch away from him.

"Hey, I was only kidding!" he called.

She didn't turn around. She knew she could get out of the house the back way through the big doors in the dining room. But where was Paul? she wondered. She looked around desperately.

At the other entrance of the living room, Paul bumped into a middle-aged man with almond-shaped eyes. He held out his hand. "I'm Paul Montclair," he said. He noted the coolness of the man's hand, but he told himself he was past shocking. "I wonder if you know my father,

Richard?" Paul asked. "He's about your age."

"I'm sorry," said the man. He had a British accent. "I'm not from around here. Try Dubay over there. He seems to know everyone." The Englishman indicated a tough-looking young man wearing tight jeans and a black T-shirt. Dubay was heavily muscular—his thighs bulged under the tight jeans. He wore an earring in one nostril. He looked far too young to be a contemporary of Paul's father, but Paul was beginning to see that with vampires age was a tricky concept since they evidently stopped maturing once they became vampires. Uncomfortably he recalled that the sexy young blonde he had been talking to must have gone to school with Sybil's mother.

Paul approached Dubay cautiously.

The man smiled. It was a careful smile Paul recognized now as typical of vampires, the sort of closed-jaw smile that didn't reveal fangs.

"I was told you might know my father, Richard Montclair," he said.

"Oh, yes," said Dubay. "I know Richard." He didn't offer any further information.

"I haven't seen him since I was little," said Paul. "I was hoping you could tell me a little about him."

"We aren't close friends," Dubay began cautiously. "Richard runs in too fast a crowd for me."

Paul regarded Dubay with dismay. What sort of crowd could be too fast for this tough-looking fellow?

Dubay aimlessly scratched the corner of his eye

with a broken thumbnail. "Why don't you ask Alain about him? He probably could tell you more than I could." Dubay put his hand on a neighboring guest's shoulder and whirled him around to face them. Alain proved to be a dark and slender young man with a cynical twist to his thin lips.

"Cut it out, Dubay!" cried Alain. "Must you be so piggishly self-centered? I mean, really!"

"Tell the young man about Richard Montclair," said Dubay. "They're related but haven't met."

"Where to begin!" cried Alain. "Richard is in a class by himself. Utterly reckless. One has to admire that. There's a kind of integrity to it, a kind of primitive magnificence."

"Do you have any idea what he does for a living?" Paul asked.

Dubay and Alain looked at him blankly. "Oh, Richard doesn't work," Alain said faintly.

Paul flushed. He felt dizzy, but somehow he managed to keep talking. "Have you seen him around lately?" he asked.

"I hear he's been around rather a lot the past few weeks. I haven't actually *seen* him—that is to say, with my own eyes. But several mutual acquaintances have run into him, and I myself was coming out of a midnight movie only a few days ago, and I heard that incredibly irritating whistle of his. Richard can't carry a tune in a bucket." The young man laughed, showing gleaming white fangs. "I'd have known that off-key whistle of his anywhere. I suppose he's probably in Bombay or Singapore as we speak. He's always had a weak spot for warm, steamy nights."

Like the nights in New Orleans, thought Paul. With sickening clarity he remembered how all those corpses in New Orleans had been drained of blood. The thought made his stomach turn over. The tuneless whistling he had heard that foggy day at the track haunted his mind—his father!

Loud music had begun to play, and the vampires swayed in time with it. Paul felt dizzy. Black velvet brushed suddenly against his cheek, and Paul looked up, startled to see jewel-colored eyes in a Nordic, square-jawed face. "Want to dance?" cooed the woman in black velvet. "I simply love to dance," she said. Her fangs glistened in the dim light as she wound a pale arm around him. To his horror, he found his body swaying and moving in time to hers. He shimmied close against her. Sweat trickled down his face, and her breath stirred his hair. He stared as if hypnotized at the triangle of one of her rhinestone earrings. Impossibly bright, the jewels dazzled him, and for an instant his vision blurred so that all he saw was a mosaic of spangled light. The music held him in its grip. His pulse had become one with its beat. The coolness of the vampire's breasts pressed against his chest horrified him, yet he could not pull away. "Having fun?" she cooed.

"Y-yes," he stuttered. The sound that came out of his mouth appalled him. He wanted to get away, didn't he? Why had he said he was having fun? He listened to his heart thump loudly in his ears. He felt cool and strangely disassociated from his hot body.

"Would you like to go out with me sometime?" she cooed. "I simply adore young boys." She seized his finger and put it in her mouth, and a shudder of dread shook him. He could feel her wet lips and he cringed, expecting to feel the prick of her fangs. Instead, a tingling sensation shot through him, as if he had touched a wet battery. Then his hand fell free and she smiled mischievously at him, showing her fangs. Paul felt like a fool. What had he thought? That she was going to suck the life-blood out of him through a single finger? The cold dampness of his finger mocked him.

"I . . . I'm sorry," he said, backing off suddenly. "I have to go."

She pursed her red lips and mouthed something, but he couldn't hear her over the loud music. She looked more sinister than sexy in that black dress, and Paul was afraid to meet her gaze. With a sudden dread, he remembered Ari. He should have stayed with her.

No wonder his mother had been drawn to his father, he thought uncomfortably, recalling the wiles of Verena and the tall vampire in black velvet. He stumbled to the dining room and poured himself another glass of wine. The room seemed stiflingly hot, and he knew he was getting drunk, but he couldn't stop himself.

He wasn't sure how long he stared out the French doors. He felt as if he were floating through a universe of stars and blackness with nothing to hold him in one place.

Ari's voice startled him. "Paul?"

Paul blinked. He hadn't seen her standing there in the shadows, her back against the French doors. "Jeez, Ari, I'm glad to see you. I've been worried about you." Guilt pricked him. He should have been protecting her, he thought. He had been shimmying with vampires when he should have been looking out for his sister.

"I thought about going out to the garden," said Ari in a small voice. "But then I started to worry. What if I met one of them out there? Or on the garden path? That would be even worse." She shuddered. "At least it's quiet here. None of them go near the food table." She peered at him closely. "Are you all right? You haven't been drinking again, have you?"

"What if I have?" he said. "I'm entitled."

Ari put her hand on his arm. "Listen," she said. "I'm counting on you. You've got to keep sober. You're all I've got!"

Suddenly Paul felt ashamed of himself. How could he feel cut adrift when he had Ari? He glanced over his shoulder down the long hallway. The music was playing softly now, and he could see that people were leaving.

"I think the party's starting to break up." Ari took a deep breath. "Good."

Paul shot her an uneasy glance. "None of those vampires gave you a hard time, did they?"

"A couple tried." Ari's eyes flashed. "But I didn't let them get away with anything."

Paul felt sick with shame. The dim thought had crept into his mind that maybe he hadn't wanted to get away from that tall blond vampire as much as he imagined. Maybe she had sensed his ambivalence and sucked up his strength.

"Did anybody else try anything with you?" asked Ari.

Paul felt himself go scarlet. "Same as with you," he said gruffly. "I fought them off." Remembering the way he had danced so close to the vampire's cold, vulpine body, he felt unclean.

Ari lowered her voice. "It's scary, though, Paul. They don't feel any pain, and they're already dead so you feel so . . . weak. And something strange happens when they touch you." The color drained from her face at the memory.

"You don't have to tell me about it," said Paul quickly. In a quick flash of comprehension, he sensed that Ari, too, despite her brave words, was badly shaken. At least, he thought, the party was breaking up.

Paul and Ari pulled up chairs to a corner of the dining room table, and comforted by the other's presence, they began companionably eating off each other's plates. "The lobster's good," said Ari after a minute.

"I'm sick of lobster." Paul gave his familiar crooked smile. "I'm sick of this whole scene." He gave Ari a sip out of his wineglass.

The elaborate buffet with its frosted grapes, its cold seafood, dip, and crackers was as symmetrical and as carefully arranged as when the caterers had left.

"I wonder what happens to all this food," Ari said.

Paul shrugged. "Donation to a soup kitchen? Compost heap? Caterer's cleanup crew gets to pig out? Dunno."

Finally, they became aware that the house had grown still. Even the music had stopped. "I bet they've gone on to other parties," said Paul. He remembered the bar he had gone into looking for Aunt Gabrielle. The woman at the bar had had fangs—he hadn't imagined it. The place must have been a vampire hangout. "I have the idea this bunch does a lot of partying," he said.

Together they tiptoed up the marble hall and peeked in the living room. Everyone was gone. Ari popped a last grape in her mouth as she sat down. "One thing about vampires," she said calmly. "No cigarette stubs all over the Oriental carpet after the party."

"Great," said Paul. "That makes it all seem worthwhile."

They heard squeals of delight and the front door closed. Aunt Gabrielle was radiant as she stepped into the dining room. "There!" she cried. "Aren't they charming? My dear, dear friends. I wanted you to see that we aren't a bunch of losers." She clasped her hands together. "I wanted you to have some real appreciation of your heritage."

Her words lay in Ari's stomach like cold stones. For the first time, it struck Ari as sinister that her name seemed to echo her aunt's—Ari, Gabri. Too close for comfort. "What do you mean, 'our heritage'?" she choked.

Aunt Gabrielle perched on the striped couch,

leaning slightly toward the twins. "My dears, haven't you noticed that you see the world in a more intense and colorful way than ordinary people?"

Ari's gaze met Paul's. She and Paul saw letters and numbers in color. Was that what Aunt Gabrielle was talking about?

"Haven't you noticed the awakening of a feeling that there's more to the world than simple everyday life?" prompted Aunt Gabrielle gently. "You have visions, perhaps. See things that other people can't see?"

Ari thought of the ghost she had seen near Sybil's house. No one else had seen it, Sybil had said. At least not for years. And the morning visions that Paul had assured her were normal. She stared at Aunt Gabrielle, appalled.

"It's a sign of the potential that's there inside you," Aunt Gabrielle went on. "You must have noticed how some families produce musicians, others mathematicians. We tend to produce vampires," she said with modest pride.

"No!" cried Ari. "I'm not a vampire." She and Paul stared at each other in dismay. Paul's hand was in his pocket on the cigarette lighter, but all of a sudden he was unsure what to do with it.

Aunt Gabrielle reached for her purse and struggled with the clasp a minute. Then she produced a gold compact and flicked it open before Ari's face so that its mirror cast a circle of light on Ari's mouth. "But you are a vampire, dearest," she cried. "See your cute little baby fangs?"

CHAPTER
NINETEEN

THE TWINS RAN UPSTAIRS ALL AT ONCE, SLAMMED THE
door, and fell into each other's arms on Ari's bed.
"It can't be true," Ari sobbed. "No! No! It can't be."

Paul stroked her hair, but a moment later the
twins found each other gazing in horrified fascina-
tion at the other's mouth, the soft pink of the
parted lips, the white gleam of teeth, and the
pointy incisors. "Whatever it is, Ari," he said,
"we're in it together. You and me. From beginning
to end, we'll never be alone."

Ari turned and pinched her arm, reassured by
its pink fleshiness. Lots of people had pointed incisors, she told herself. It didn't mean she and Paul
were vampires. But she knew that she was changing. Every week she felt stronger and more grown
up. Was she somehow also changing into a vampire without realizing it? "How can we be the children of a vampire?" she cried. "Vampires can't

have children. They don't have sex. They aren't even alive."

"I've thought about that," said Paul. "Maybe our parents got together before Dad became a vampire."

Ari jumped up from the bed and began pacing tight circles on the floor. "I don't feel a bit like a vampire, do you? The sun doesn't bother me. I don't even like my steak rare!"

Paul regarded her cautiously. "Maybe it's just that the tendency runs in the family," he said. "Some families have a lot of musicians or scientists. Stands to reason all of them aren't musicians or scientists. Some of them end up working in convenience stores, right? Nothing is a hundred percent. Maybe we'll be the lucky ones who don't make it as vampires."

Tears streamed down Ari's cheeks. "I'm scared, Paul. Maybe we're turning every minute. Maybe we're already becoming vampires."

A clap of thunder sounded. The floor trembled and the prisms of the bedside lamp jingled. Ari ran to the window and threw it open. A wind blew in, ruffling her hair. A sheet of paper was swept to the floor. Ari heard a rustling sound and knew without turning around that the fanged creatures were in the room. They were nosing in her things while her back was turned.

"Ari?" She could hear Paul's voice coming as if from a great distance, but she couldn't turn around. She stared out the window in a trance.

A black cloud rose before her, swallowing up

the terrace below in a roar, and the hot sweep of wind brushed against her cheeks. Flames licked at the brick buildings of the courtyard, and through the flames she saw a dark figure in a cape on the fire escape of the tall building behind the terrace. Somewhere people were shouting and Ari heard the sound of sirens. Bits of ash floated aimlessly in the air. The dark man's cape was swept out balloon-style by the holocaust of fire, and someone screamed. Ari's flesh crawled. Through the flames, she could see that blood was streaming down the buildings. It lay in pools on the terrace.

"No!" Ari cried. She squeezed her eyes closed and covered her ears. "It's not going to happen to me. I won't let it. No! Never!"

"Ari? Are you okay?" She felt Paul's arms around her. Ari turned to meet his gaze and felt her heartbeat slowing down and becoming more steady.

"Paul," she sobbed, "something horrible's about to happen."

"Something horrible's always about to happen," he said wearily. "We can't worry about that right now. We've got to figure out what to do."

Ari gazed out the window once more and saw that the fire and the blood were gone. She gulped for air. It had been a vision, she knew. But it had been so real—like a window into the future.

"Paul," said Ari in a calmer voice. "The man is still there. The one that was on the fire escape in my vision."

"What man?" Paul peered out the window. A

229

black-caped figure stepped across the petunias and walked deliberately across the bricked pavement of the terrace. So foreshortened was the figure below that they saw only a suggestion of white face and white—gloves, perhaps?—against the black of darkness, clothes, and cape.

Ari held Paul's arm in a tight grip. "It's our father."

A chill slithered up Paul's spine. "Maybe not," he said.

A tuneless whistle floated up to them as the doors of Aunt Gabrielle's study were thrown open.

"He's come for us," cried Ari. "He's going to make us into vampires."

Paul had an uncomfortable flashback to the girl at the party. She wanted to mix her blood with his. Suddenly Paul was sure Ari was right. Their father was going to make them into vampires so they would be with him forever.

"I won't let him!" cried Ari. She slammed the window shut and fastened the catch. "Lock the doors, Paul."

Paul leapt to the connecting door and slid its lock into place. He heard Ari turn the big key in the door to the hall. She took the key out of the lock and dropped it on the floor.

"The bathroom," she said breathlessly. "I'll get the window. Then we'll be locked in. We've got water. We can last in here a long time."

Paul was miserably conscious of the flimsiness of the latch on the connecting doors. The lock to the hall door was sturdier, but he doubted that either door would stand up if a grown man threw his weight against the frame.

Ari spoke in a low trembling voice. "Don't let him talk you into anything, Paul. We don't open those doors no matter what, do you hear me? Promise!"

Paul nodded.

They heard rapid heavy footfalls in the hallway, and suddenly the door rattled with heavy and insistent banging. Someone was trying the doorknob. "Open up!" someone muttered. The frame of the door shuddered as a heavy weight was thrown against it. Paul heard the splintering of wood and gazed at Ari in terror.

VAMPIRE TWINS 1

BLOODLINES

To be continued…look out for
Vampire Twins 2 Bloodlust

Come a Stranger
by Cynthia Voigt £3.50

For Mina, the scholarship to Ballet School summer camp was the most marvellous experience in her life. But in her second year she is ungainly and clumsy and after only a few weeks she is asked to leave. Mina thinks she has been rejected because she is black and her once sunny world is clouded with uncertainty.

Sons from Afar
by Cynthia Voigt £3.50

James and Sammy Tillerman's father walked out when they were very young, so long ago that Sammy can't understand why James is interested in him. But James desperately needs to find out what kind of man his father was.

Seventeen Against the Dealer
by Cynthia Voigt £3.50

The final book in the Tillerman saga. Dicey is now trying to earn her own living as a boatbuilder despite demands made on her by her family. A drifter turns up at the workshop offering his help, and Dicey comes to trust him, letting him work with her and enjoying his company. But problems at home and at work overwhelm her, and she ends up trusting him too much.

Sweet Goodbyes

A wonderful series of heart-rending stories that will make you cry. Ordinary high-school girls are suddenly forced to cope with a life-threatening illness. Things will never be the same again, as each girl fights to survive...

Please Don't Go
Losing David
Life Without Alice
My Sister, My Sorrow
Goodbye, Best Friend
The Dying of the Light

All at £2.99

Order Form

To order direct from the publishers, just make a list of the titles you want and fill in the form below:

Name ....

Address ....

....

....

Send to: Dept 6, HarperCollins Publishers Ltd, Westerhill Road, Bishopbriggs, Glasgow G64 2QT.

Please enclose a cheque or postal order to the value of the cover price, plus:

UK & BFPO: Add £1.00 for the first book, and 25p per copy for each addition book ordered.

Overseas and Eire: Add £2.95 service charge. Books will be sent by surface mail but quotes for airmail despatch will be given on request.

A 24-hour telephone ordering service is avail-able to Visa and Access card holders: 041-772 2281